Sentinel

by Laura J Carter

First published in the United Kingdom in 2020 by
Wobbly Press
©2020 Laura J Carter

ISBN 978-0-9955109-4-4

www.wobblypress.co.uk

For Elin

Contents

1

The Cottage

It was because of the argument that she was here. The wet wood smell followed her as she emerged onto the meadow. Out in the open. Looking hard at the problem trainers, soaked through to her socks.

Stupid shoes. Stupid socks.

A drip fell onto the shoulder of her coat, making a darker patch of red. She fiddled with the familiar hole in her pocket, balling the threads with her thumb and forefinger. Breathing in, Lucy let the cold air mist out again from her lips in a long cloud that melted into the trees behind her.

Mum called out from the fence. Lucy imagined her leaning against it with her arms huddled over her favourite green scarf from Liberty's, and with cold showing pink on her cheeks. She hadn't been past the fence since her heel got stuck in a tree root.

A rabbit scuffled nearby, then darted out of a hawthorn, tail bouncing. Rabbits didn't have to wear shoes. Or visit shoe shops. They were oblivious to growing older. Changing. 'Transitioning to adulthood'. Lucy had seen that written on a file once, when the doctor had assumed she couldn't read yet and had left it open on his desk.

She withdrew a pad of sticky notes and a tiny biro from her jeans. The biro had been from a street stall in Spain. She remembered the acrid sweat smell, mixed in with suntan cream and spilled chips. The smell memory was always there, as though it was somehow trapped inside with the ink.

Do rabbits know how old they are?

She wrote it precisely, without joining up, and slid it back into its usual place where the corners had made lighter patches in the denim. Mum had given her a notebook for Christmas. It had rabbits on the cover. And fairies. Pink fluffy things with sickly glitter lips and hovering insects in their hair. The paper rabbits looked up at their wings with shiny eyes. Flat and stiff. Lucy had left the book on her bedside table so that it looked like she was using it. It was under her clock.

"Lucy! Where are you?"

She stepped to the left and onto a polished root. This was in the direct eyeline of the gap in the fence where the path started, so Mum could see her. Well, the back of her jeans, anyway. Six seconds later, the back door of the cottage slammed.

The rabbit stopped at the top of the slope and looked back. Ears up, twitching. Watching. The root dug comfortingly into the arches of Lucy's feet and pushed her toes further forward. Her toenails ached wonderfully at the end of her safe old shoes.

Taking slow measured breaths, she closed her eyes. She concentrated on the breeze, its tiny cold fingers exploring the pores in her skin. The smell was amazing here. Grass, dirt, trees, realness. Sturdiness. Calm.

When she opened them, she saw something else on the hill. It wasn't another rabbit, it was bigger than that. The legs seemed to be much longer and set in front as it sat on its haunches. The ears were tall and tipped with black. Cheeks defined. She could see that even from that distance. It was calmly looking at her. Big eyes looking straight at her. Through her. They locked her gaze, but it didn't hurt, not like with people. It seemed to acknowledge her with a slight nod, only to then turn and disappear over the brow of the hill. The air around her seemed to pause, and Lucy had a feeling the creature was female, and old. Very old. She had no idea why she knew, the idea just appeared in her head. Her shoulders dropped, and she started breathing again, not realising she had stopped. The sky was greying, and more dark patches were blossoming on her coat. Lucy turned and headed back down the path.

"I think I saw a hare, Mum."

"Mmhmm."

"It looked at me."

"Lovely, darling."

The laptop's glow made the air crackle near Lucy's earlobes. She looked away. Mum was obviously zoned into a work thing. Only a fire alarm would get through to her.

Lucy hung her coat on the banister and made her way upstairs, her footsteps releasing the musty smell of a little used, but very old, carpet.

Her new room looked over the garden, and you could see the path to the woods, smeared by the old glass in their tiny rectangles. There was still a large cardboard packing box in one corner, even after three weeks. Her things didn't belong in this room yet, didn't have a place.

There was calm here, though. Still lots going on, but the noise was different. The old radiator gurgled. The trees rustled. The house creaked when the temperature dropped at night, and the birdsong varied according to the time of day. Sometimes a tractor went past, sometimes with a trailer banging and bouncing behind. The noises were just better, less angry than London noises, where everyone was rushing, and the crowds seemed to follow you home and stay with you, knocking on your brain, trying to get in.

The front door clicked open and shut with a slight 'whump', keys on the hook, bag dumped in the hall. Muffled conversation, and the sound of the kettle being put on. Danny's trainers scuffed up the stairs and he rapped on her door frame.

"All right, freakoid?"

Lucy smiled at the wall.

"I hear you've been giving Mum some jip about your shoes again." He chucked a bag of M&Ms on her bed. "Cheer up, Mucka."

Lucy grinned at his chin, catching his eye oh so briefly, not realising how hungry she was. The green ones were her favourite. They reminded her of the park she used to go to with him as a toddler. They used to sit on the same bench and watch the 'yummy mummy' runners sail past in their designer Lycra. And Danny used to go on about the band he was going to set up, and the tours to America, and that when he was famous, he would buy her a lifetime supply of only green M&Ms. They would have to be special order.

"Thanks, Danny."

Danny stomped to his room, replacing his headphones as he went, and mouthing the words to a song in a ridiculously high rasp. His bed creaked, and the familiar strumming of his guitar wheedled its way through the wall. He'd obviously had a good day out with his girlfriend. Things had been a bit rocky since they'd moved. He had to take a bus and two trains now, so he could only see her on weekends. Ros called her a freak as well, but not like Danny did. Meanwhile, the new shoes stared at her from a space by the door.

2

The Yew

Puck knelt in the wet grass and felt the ground seethe beneath him. The earth was always more active here. The incantations used to keep the area secure always set the creatures a little on edge. The beetles were more frantic, and the birds flew haphazardly even when the wind was slight.

The Yew was silent, unmoving. A sense of foreboding in the ancient boughs reached out above his head. He remembered when the tree was a mere forty years old, just a youth, when the first spells were cast and the responsibility of keeping the hill under strict surveillance was set. He closed his eyes and sunk his fingers into sweet soil. He found the pulse immediately, making his arm twitch and his breath quicken. Even after all these years… The power of this place. It sang through his veins.

"You got my message, then."

Puck's eyes opened to see a pair of Wellington boots caked in mud. The edge of a grimy coat brushed the rubber tops. Same frayed hems and bleached thread.

"I came immediately, Ceinwen." Puck rose to his feet and stood tall, still only to the shoulder of the woman who was rooted to the ground in front of him, despite his more extensive years.

"Just as bloody well, Sprite. You lot have left me here too long. I warned you this would happen." The woman's fists were firmly in pockets, and her hair hung down, stalwart.

"You are aware there was a war, there has been work to—"

The woman laughed loud and hard. The sound reverberated through the branches above her and the bark seemed to curl and ripple.

"That finished in 1945. I know, I was there. May I remind you who we are keeping here."

She was right, of course. The Council had concentrated solely on the repair of the land and protection of the all the species harmed in those years. It wasn't just the two great wars that had caused havoc with the Balance, it was everything since then. Munitions dumps seeping into ancient magical pathways, extensive building on sacred land, not to mention the stripping of resources, and constant pollutants coming from the ever-expanding population of people. The Council had neglected the hill, he knew that. It wasn't a patch on what the Europeans had had to deal with this last century, but still…

"Please accept my apologies, Ceinwen, I am here now."

The old woman's grey eyes gazed unmoving. The boughs creaked, and the soil beneath his bare feet simmered. A deliberate time passed. A truce hung between them.

"I have a batch of blackberry wine at the house."

"Thank you. I shall be delighted to try a glass."

They turned to traverse the hill, his bare soles sensing every stalk of grass and writhing insect, her boots striding out long. Neither walker left footprints.

3

The Fair

"They are exactly the same, Lucy." Mum's exasperation was barely hidden. She crossed her arms. "I trawled the Internet for those damn shoes."

They weren't the same. They looked the same, but they just weren't. They were stiff, and there was too much space by her toes. Her socks slid around inside. They were just…

Wrong.

Mum let out her breath, seeming to count in her head like she always had.

"Promise me you'll try them, Lucy. Please?"

She nodded and Mum turned towards the stairs. Lucy slid the Post-it Notes out of her pocket and wrote, 'Growth rate of feet. Rabbits/hares?' The corners were starting to curl. She would have to ask Danny to get her another pack.

"You'll need your coat, Lucy, it's spitting." Mum called as she slid her rings down the banister. They dragged along the wood with an excruciating scrape.

Lucy looked at the new shoes, and then slid her old ones out from under her bed. They were going to a fair. She would need something familiar to concentrate on.

She shrugged on her red coat, stuck her finger through the hole in her pocket, took a deep breath, and made her way downstairs.

Danny was waiting by the door with his hand on the edge by the ancient lock. The tips of his fingers were rough, and Lucy could hear them rubbing on the wood as he opened the door wider to let her through.

"C'mon, Luce, it won't be that bad. Mum needs this."

Lucy looked at his chin, nodded and then stepped out onto the doorstep. Danny clicked the door shut behind them. No escape now.

Their tiny town car tyres bumped over a rutted field towards a skinny teen in a DayGlo orange jacket. He pointed to his left, looking bored. Mum tipped her head in thanks and they crawled next to a far too clean Land Rover. Lucy watched as an estate pulled up next to them with three kids in the back and a boot full of child paraphernalia. The dad's hair was messy, and he had a creased shirt on.

"Right then." Mum turned to face her in the back seat. "Stick close to Danny, if you get lost, head for the beer tent and I'll meet you there." Lucy nodded. Danny was texting.

"Mmhmm."

"Danny, did you hear that? You stay with Luce, OK?"

Mum opened her door and her stiletto immediately sunk into the ground. She sighed.

"Here goes nothing…"

She put on her 'approachable and professional' face, grabbed her handbag, and set off at a pace, leaving Danny and Lucy to hurry after her.

The fair loomed larger and larger. The smell of the damp grass, steaming in the spring sun, combined with sickly sweet ice cream, frying doughnuts and diesel generators. There was a hint of fresh cow pat, and the familiar sweaty waft from a large group of people. Somewhere, a gruff voice was singing what might have been a country song, accompanied by a drummer who was brushing a symbol slightly out of synch. A jaunty announcement emanated from a large speaker at the entrance, relaying that the winner of this morning's 'Dog who looks most like their owner' competition had been won by none other than Mr Brown and his miniature Schnauzer, Patsy.

As they entered a tent open at both ends and with fold up tables on each side, locals in wax jackets and brimmed hats smiled and held out programmes.

"Ferret racing is at two thirty, vintage vehicles at 3:00 p.m., and the cheese judging is starting in ten minutes," volunteered a particularly tall chap with a moustache and hairy earlobes. "And look at that, it's stopped raining!"

Lucy stared at the earlobes. The hairs were as long as her fingernails and they curled around to the back. The wax jackets smelled damp and chemically and her throat tightened.

"Oh, how wonderful!" Mum smiled at him and offered her recently manicured hand. "We're new to the village, so we're looking forward to sampling the local delights." She winked at him as he took her hand and bowed his head slightly.

"Pleasure to meet you, Mrs, er?"

"Ms"

"Oh, er…"

"Ms Chatham, Chatham Events. Very pleased to make your acquaintance, Mr?"

"Dr Cooke. I'm afraid I'm moonlighting as a helper today."

"Simply fantastic!" Mum gave her a glance with wide eyes which meant 'stop staring' and she followed the earlobes, and their owner, into the sun on the other side of the tent. Mum was using her posh voice and a smile that was so wide you could see her fillings. It made her look a bit manic. Lucy looked up at the bright sun and wondered what on earth the 'moonlighter' was talking about.

Danny shoved his phone into his jeans, balled his fists into his jacket pockets and grinned. "Right'o, freak, let's see what *delights* the village fair has to offer, shall we?"

Lucy took a deep breath and followed him into the fray.

Along a trodden strip of grass, in between numerous stalls, were people selling various wares ranging from homemade chutneys and jams, sausages, and cheese, to carved wooden toddler toys and antique furniture. They strolled past a plant stall where a man was wrestling a huge spiked bush into a plastic bag at the same time as answering a question about whether a hydrangea could grow in full sun. There was constant chatter, and laughter trickled.

Danny stopped by a van whose sign said it sold 'The Best Coffee in the Village'. Rich caffeine aromas wafted out, making the air thick. Lucy took short breaths so as to not let too much in.

"Ooh, I could do with one of them," he said, eyeing the pastries on offer. "You want anything?"

Lucy forced a smile. "Coke?"

"On it."

Danny joined the queue while Lucy loitered near the plant stall, accidentally brushing her hand on a lavender which released the musky scent of the flowers. Her nose tickled. It was getting hotter now the rain had stopped, and the back of her neck itched. As her eyes wandered through the crowd, she saw a woman looking in her direction. She was Lucy's height, with an ancient coat and Wellington boots, and long hair tied in a rough bun at the back. Wisps escaped and hung down by her face. She was both young and old at the same time. Her back was straight, as ballet dancers stand when they're not on stage. Naturally holding a posture, always ready for the orchestra to start playing.

The crowds seemed to walk around her without acknowledgment, as though she were a rock in a ploughed field, and she was staring straight at Lucy.

Something cold touched her palm. Looking down, Lucy found a can of Coke, wet with condensation.

"I went for a Mocca Chocca Latte with extra drizzle! Wanna try some?" Danny had foam on his top lip and both hands wrapped around a takeaway cup.

"No thanks. Can you see that woman?"

Lucy pointed, but the woman had vanished. She looked up and down the tented alleyway but couldn't see anyone looking remotely like the person she'd seen.

"Come on, Luce, let's go and see who's murdering that guitar, shall we?"

"Erm. OK." She followed him, trying to avoid brushing arms with shoppers.

They stood and watched the band for a bit, Lucy gritting her teeth and flinching occasionally at passers by. Danny made comments in her ear about how terrible they were and made her giggle, despite herself. Then his phone rang.

He took it out of his pocket, looking at the caller ID. He took a deep breath in and combed his fingers through his hair.

"It's Ros. Better take it." He looked at Lucy apologetically and turned towards the main thoroughfare. Lucy watched him for a while. He started to gesticulate and shake his head. Lucy turned back to the stage. She hated seeing him upset. The band was performing what passed as some sort of finale as, agitated, she rubbed her fingers around the loose stitching in her pocket.

The estate car family made their way towards a picnic bench a few feet away. The dad's shirt was billowing out at the back and he had a large pink hold-all that had stuff spilling out of one of the pockets. He had a toddler on his arm and two younger kids running circles around his legs.

He hefted his load onto the other hip and chucked the bag on the table, sitting down with a large exhale of breath, and got out a couple of water bottles with cartoon dogs on them. The two children were now doing circuits around the table. One banged his head on a corner and started wailing. Lucy took a few steps away as discretely as she could. The noise was making the bit behind her eyeballs buzz.

The band had finished their song, and there was an abrupt squeal as the lead singer put the microphone too close to a speaker. Lucy darted her palms onto her ears. Two blokes near the stage jeered at him loudly and started whistling, the loud kind where people use their fingers to push their tongue. Lucy gritted her teeth tighter, closing her eyes. Her heart was starting to beat against her ribs.

A couple walked past with an Alsatian who started barking at the whistlers. The toddler was howling now, and the smell of frying wafted and made vomit gather in the back of her throat. The Alsatian owner was yelling at the dog and people were looking in her direction as she started to bounce on her toes, hands still on her ears. The mum from the estate emerged from the side and put her hand on Lucy's arm, making all the hairs stand up under her coat. The skin on her shoulder seemed to fizz.

"You all right, love?"

Lucy bolted.

She headed for the gate but saw her mum and hairy-earlobe-man chatting to another woman in tweed, so she veered right towards a large marquee. She couldn't let Mum see her like this, not now. She could hear someone calling out her name, but she couldn't stop, she had to hide, recover. Her heart was pounding, and she could feel her muscles straining against her clothes as she ran full pelt. There was the heavy scent of animals. She dashed through the entrance and found herself among metal pens. Most had sheep, pigs, or calves, but over in the corner to her left were some empty ones. She sprang over the fence and crouched behind a bale of hay. Arms round her knees, she closed her eyes and squeezed herself as tightly as she could. Deep breaths, Lucy, deep breaths. She rocked herself gently and inhaled the fragrance of the hay, sweet and musty. A calf a few pens away lowed and shifted its weight, making its bedding rustle and a puff of dust rise. The child's cry was still ringing in her ears and the reek of frying fat had followed her. Deep breaths. In. Out. In. Out. Back and forth, back and forth. Her heart was slowing a little now. Back and forth, back and forth. She released her knees and felt for the hole in her pocket. It was still there. She stuck her finger through it.

"I can't understand it, Arthur. She got a first last year. Can't believe that woman from Clacketts farm, the cheek of… Aah! What the…?"

A large lady in a white coat loomed over Lucy. She was holding the lead of a very clean goat with a 'highly commended' rosette on the collar.

"What the bloody hell are you doing in there? Visitors aren't allowed inside the pens. Anyway, what possessed you to—"

Lucy put her hands back over her ears and closed her eyes again. She started humming. The woman put her hands round Lucy's wrist. She wrenched it away and hummed louder, trying to drown out the world.

"What a rude girl! You just wait til I find ya parents young lady… Can you believe it, Arthur! We can't put our Rosy in 'ere with 'er."

A small crowd was beginning to gather around the pen, and the woman in the white coat was getting louder, obviously enjoying the audience. Lucy opened one eye and immediately shut it again. Back and forth, back and forth, in, out, in, out. There was a shuffle of feet and the low mutter of onlookers. Lucy could feel their stares on her skin like a bright light. She knew their arms would be crossed, and their heads would be shaking, and there would be the comments she recognised so well. *What's she rocking for? Summat wrong with 'er. Where're the parents? Disgraceful behaviour! Tantrum. Rude girl...* They came, as she knew they would. Did they not realise there was nothing she could do? She hummed louder and struck her back against the metal pen as she rocked. She sensed the warmth of another body near her.

"What's your name, honey?" Arthur had bent down. His voice was low and gravelly, and he smelled of breath mints.

Lucy couldn't answer him. She really wanted to, but she just couldn't. Her words were stuck in her chest somewhere. She wanted to say, 'get Danny', but even when she opened her lips slightly, nothing came out. She brought her knees up to her face and rested her forehead on them, hoping with all her might that he could hear her thoughts, somehow.

Then, there he was. He was breathing fast like he'd been running, and he leaned down and filled the space. "It's OK, Luce, I'm here. I'm so sorry. Come on, Luce. It's OK."

He turned to the group of people and looked directly at them, his eyes saying exactly what he thought of them and their disapproval.

"It's all right, she's with me." He looked harder and waited, saying nothing, until they'd got the hint.

They dispersed, tutting. The goat woman stayed by, muttering to the space the crowd had vacated, but her husband shushed her.

"Can you get up, Luce?"

Lucy couldn't move. She kept her eyes closed and shook her head. Not yet. Just, not yet. Back and forth, back and forth.

"OK, we'll stay a while longer."

Danny sat down on the floor next to her. Not touching, but she could feel the heat from his thigh.

"I'm here, Luce. Take as long as you need."

4

The Meadow

"Well, that was a great introduction to my potential customers," Mum said as she closed the car door behind her a little firmer than necessary. "I asked you to stick with her, Danny. What the hell happened?"

Danny stared out the window.

"I was, Mum."

"Well, it's pretty clear you weren't."

"Well, she's your bloody daughter!"

"Don't you dare use that tone, Danny. I'm doing my best here."

"I've got my own life to live, Mum, despite your efforts to destroy it."

Danny opened his door and got out, slamming it behind him.

"I'll walk," he mouthed through the window.

"Fine." Mum turned the key in the ignition, crunched the gears and moved off.

Lucy melted into her hood, playing with the hole in her pocket. Her cheeks were still damp. She'd ruined everything. Again.

The car journey was silent. Mum breathed through her nose noisily all the way back, not saying a word. They pulled up next to the cottage and she got out, pausing before she came around to the passenger side to let Lucy out of the back, pulling the lever for the front seat and then stepping aside.

Lucy got out slowly, looking at the ground. Mum unlocked the front door, but Lucy just couldn't be inside. Not here, not now. She headed round the back, through the fence and up her path.

"Lucy, where are…"

She kept walking. Needing to be far away.

"Luce, come back. It wasn't your fault. I shouldn't have made you…" Her voice faded as Lucy skittered around the corner of the house, making the path spit gravel.

Climbing the incline through the trees and over the now familiar roots and stones, she picked her way through the fronds of bracken at the edge and out onto the meadow, where the grass had been nibbled down by generations of rabbits. She heard Mum slam the car door. Striding up the hill, Lucy felt her leg muscles ache and her breathing become heavier. The greenness was in her lungs, and with every step away from the cottage, she felt a little freer. She headed towards the lone Yew that she had seen before from a distance, standing at the highest point of the hill. As she came closer to the tree, she realised just how big it was, looming up into the sky, straight and proud. She'd not been this close before.

Heart pounding, she turned to look back the way she'd run. A wide view of fields and copses. A couple of tiny houses surrounded by miniature hedges. The cottage, with its wonky roof and forlorn paintwork. It reminded her of a train set she was shown a few years ago, fake-looking with its twee country lanes and wooden signposts pointing to places with ridiculous names.

The breeze tousled her hair and her hood fell back. Fingers of cold air touched her neck and gently nudged down the back of her t-shirt. Her cheeks were dry now, and the tightness in her chest had released with the burst of exercise, allowing her to breathe deeper and slower. The tree behind her creaked, leaves rustled, and swathes of grass tumbled and danced like waves caught by wind on a lake. She closed her eyes again and drew in the woody smell.

When she opened them she saw the hare. It was a little way off, sitting on its haunches, ears straight up, fully facing towards her and staring. The eyes bore into her like they had before. Curious.

Lucy took a step towards it and immediately slipped, tumbling one leg out in front and onto the ground, painfully jarring her elbow as she tried to catch herself. Her knee twisted and she cried out, rolling onto her side. Embarrassed, she massaged her elbow and knee and sat up. Why embarrassed? Because of the hare? She shook her head, "Don't be daft, Luce," she mumbled.

The hare had gone anyway, obviously startled by her clumsiness.

Then she noticed her right shoe. The sole had completely ripped away, the body of it dangling comically from her ankle.

"Damn!" The image of the new shoes sitting threateningly beside her chest of drawers appeared in her brain.

Taking off both shoes and shoving the ripped-off sole into her coat pocket, she pulled her hood over her hair. Today was not going well. She'd angered her mum, got her brother into trouble, and now this? She pulled at her socks too. At least she could stop those getting damp. The chilly fingers that had explored her clothing now ventured between her toes and up her jeans. Lucy shivered.

A cloud passed over the sun and the air suddenly became icy. Lucy looked down towards the cottage and instantly saw several fairy circles. Why hadn't she noticed them before? Petite white mushrooms, bald and stout, pushed up from the earth. The circles varied in size and covered the meadow. Dotted white lines meandered through the emerald grass, joining together to make rings. The air inside them seemed to shimmer, as though heat rose from within.

Weird. She stood up.

The moment her feet touched the ground her whole body spasmed. Tongues of electricity spread into every vein. She gasped, and instinctively turned to look at the tree. The bark was moving. Moving? Yes, moving like ripples in a muddy puddle, the deep lines squirming around each other. A branch seemed to be reaching towards her, spiked fingers creaking. The earth under her feet was vibrating. She could feel it thrumming on her skin.

She fled. Down the slope, feet sliding and shoes bumping in her hand. With each step her feet met with electricity, pulsing up her legs. It was bad enough that they felt too free, too open, but this was more than just the feeling of grass on her soles—this was something else. There was something in this meadow, something in the ground. Maybe it was some chemical sprayed on it or a poisonous plant; her mind was racing with ideas. As she ran past the fairy circles, the shimmering air inside had dark patches. Ghostly figures danced and writhed, there but not there. Lucy's stomach felt as if it would escape through her throat. Every limb was throbbing, and her feet stung. What was happening? She reached the edge of the meadow and the compacted soil path to the cottage. As she bounded down it, sharp bits of gravel and twigs dug into her feet, scraping the skin and making the pads sore. She hammered on the back door of the cottage.

"Lucy, what's wrong?" Her Mum's panicked face loomed through the glass as she wrestled with the key.

"I…I… The meadow… Erm …" Lucy stammered, "There's something up there."

"What? What kind of thing? What are you talking about?"

"Like a feeling, coming from the ground. It was weird. It went cold and the tree moved."

"What?" Her Mum's face changed, turning impatient. "Is this that wonderful imagination of yours running wild again?"

"No, Mum, it went through my feet. It…it was really weird, like electricity or something."

Mum put her hands on her hips. "Come on, let's go and have a look. What's going on with your shoes? Slip your wellies on."

Lucy hated her wellies, but decided this was not the time to argue. And anyway, there was no way she was putting her bare feet on that grass again. She shoved her socks back on and put her toes into the wellies. They felt awful. Empty and cold. Her toes felt like they were in a damp cave. Lucy gritted her teeth.

"Show me where you were."

They both headed up the path. Mum's shoes were wobbling all over the place, but this was the first time she'd gone right to the top. Lucy led her to her usual root and then stopped.

"Up there, near the tree."

The grass waves slowly tumbled and the clouds made shadow patches. At the summit of the hill, the tree stood still. All sense of foreboding had gone, and a blackbird chirruped from a nearby branch.

"Are you sure, Luce? I can't see anything. It looks normal."

"There were fairy circles. You know…those rings of mushrooms." Lucy didn't understand how so much could have changed in just a few minutes. Had she dreamed it?

The fairy circles had disappeared, and the bright meadow was as pretty as it normally was. She took her left foot out of a welly and tentatively poked her toe onto the edge of a tussock. Nothing.

"Something happened, Mum, definitely. I'm not lying."

"I know, love. I think maybe you might have had a bit of a daydream, though?" Mum looked at her, worry showing on her face, but also the tiredness that never really went away. "Let's go and put the kettle on. After this afternoon I think we could both do with a cup, don't you think?"

Lucy wanted to say something else but wasn't sure what. Electricity from the grass? Moving bark? Disappearing mushroom circles? Maybe eating all those green M&Ms were starting to affect her brain.

"Come on, Luce." Mum smiled, but it didn't reach her eyes. They turned and headed back to the cottage. "Well you've got no choice on trying the new shoes now, have you?"

Lucy decided not to comment.

5

The Newcomer

Ceinwen poured the dark liquid into two mismatching sherry glasses and held one out to Puck. There was dirt under her fingernails.

"Thank you."

The house was as he remembered. Dingy. Tired curtains let light in through bare patches. There was a stained blanket thrown over the armchair, and a wooden legged sofa which had seen better days. There was a radio on the table and a copper kettle on a cast iron stove. He took a sip from his glass and listened to the melancholic drip, drip, drip from the ancient tap.

"I saw a newcomer at the fair." Ceinwen sat heavily into the armchair and slugged almost her entire glass at once. "She seemed different."

"Different how?" The wine was taking effect after just one sip. A slight fuzziness behind his eyes, and a sickly-sweet coating in his throat. Puck placed his glass on the table.

"Not sure. Just different."

She fiddled with a hole in the blanket that had obviously been made larger by this same motion over many years, and her eyes wandered around the room.

"She saw me, even when I didn't want her to. Looked straight at me. I think she's sensitive. Saw her in the meadow, too. She must have moved into the old Cherry Cottage."

"Do you think she knows?"

Ceinwen laughed loud, making her cough. Puck could hear the phlegm in her throat.

"She's human. She won't know a thing. Humans stopped thinking about us centuries ago. It's all computer games and clever-phones and aeroplanes now. They won't believe in nothin' unless it's on one of them screens they're always attached to. If she's sensitive, she'll be wondering what the bloody hell's going on."

"Do you think she has anything to do with the circles failing?"

"No! I think you know what's causing it, Sprite. The world has become an angry place. People choose any old thing to start the hate. He's growing stronger. He's flexing his limbs. If we don't strengthen the circles, he'll break through. Once he's through, all hell'll break loose."

Puck, who had risked taking another sip of the potent contents of his glass, gulped too quickly and spluttered.

"Gwyllgi?"

"Of course, Gwyllgi. Him and his lackeys have been muttering. I can hear them through the barrier. They're plotting something."

"But they cannot break it. Break through, I mean? The Council set the strongest spells they had."

"Yes, but that was years ago. The time after the great wars was one of kindness and sharing. Making do and not being greedy. At least for a while. The magic has lessened over time, and what with the last fifty years of the human world making some pretty tragic decisions, he's had a lot to feed on."

"I didn't think he could feed through the barrier."

"Well he's getting stronger, whatever the reason is. You know my powers are limited. I'm not young anymore, and while I've got more common sense than you lot, I'm afraid I won't be able to hold him long if Gwyllgi decides to try and get out." She swigged the remainder of her wine and fiddled with the stem of the empty glass.

"This is serious, Ceinwen. The Balance would tip."

"Too bloody right it's serious." Moistening her lips with a stained tongue, she released a breathy sigh. "Why do you think I summoned you?"

Puck sighed. Ceinwen was right, of course. Gwyllgi was an old power. One that was very dangerous, but forgotten by most. Puck had had many discussions with the Council, who believed him to be a harmless old spirit. They were too young to understand. Too young to remember. They, like the humans, had forgotten their own history with each generation. Once, he'd had great influence over them, but now…

He was surprised when, looking down at his glass, he found it empty. If what Ceinwen had said about this meadow was true, then the battle to get the Council to be proactive was just the start.

6

The Call

"I'm lost, Mum."

Lucy paused on the stairs, left foot hovering above the creak on the third one down. She was after a glass of water after the usual hour of not being able to sleep. Mum was sitting at the kitchen table with her back to the door, phone hanging from her bent wrist, and her other hand balling a tissue. A half empty bottle of wine stood next to a glass, misty with finger and lip prints.

Lucy sat down silently with her hands under her knees, pressing her feet onto the step edge. She wanted to rock, but stopped herself automatically, even though no one was watching.

"I feel so alone. I'm stuck out here in the countryside. The locals look at me as though I'm an alien because I don't own a wax jacket."

Lucy tried to work out what Grandma was saying on the other end. She was probably in her mustard yellow armchair, and probably had her pink china teacup precariously balanced on the arm. Petula would be sprawled on her lap drooling as Grandma scratched behind her ear, leaving stiff grey hairs on her lilac dressing gown.

"But that's the problem, Mum, I didn't fit in in Islington either. Do you remember that Sylvia? She used to cross the road to avoid us. Cross the road! Her and her brat. Stupid woman."

Lucy started picking at the skin around her nails. This conversation was familiar. She'd heard it before, although Mum didn't know she had.

"I've given up everything, my beautiful town house, my career, my savings, my friends..."

Mum's friends hadn't bothered to call her. The last one had come to look at the new house, made some comment about it being quaint and a bit remote and then left, having not removed her coat.

"Yes, they were my friends, Mum, until Sylvia wheedled her way in and told them I'd paid for that diagnosis just to get attention. Like she'd know how hard it was to get one. That NHS doc said six years on a waiting list, although to be honest I'm not sure there was ever any point anyway. It still didn't get her any help, did it?"

Lucy's dad had left about the same time, about a year ago. He was very annoyed when Mum decided to move out here. He kept giving Lucy art sets. Pencils and stuff, like she was going to suddenly reproduce a photographic drawing of some building like that boy on the telly. He hadn't visited them at the cottage yet. Lucy wasn't sure he ever would.

"And that meet up I went to, when that boy spat at me. Told me that my 'cohort' should be locked up for what we're doing to our children. I thought I could learn from them, Mum, I thought I would be able to understand what Lucy needed when she's in her teens, or later on. I'm not always going to be around, Mum. I need to set things up."

Mum gulped some wine and rubbed the back of her neck. She looked much smaller than usual. Lucy stepped heavily onto the creaky step and padded down the stairs, not wishing to hear any more. A glass was by the sink ready for her, as always. She filled it about three quarters of the way up, swigged three mouthfuls and then refilled it to the same imaginary line. She padded more slowly past the table and glanced at the wine bottle. It was almost empty.

"You OK, Lucy? Can't sleep again?"

Lucy couldn't manage to look at her Mum, although her heart was wrenching to. She'd done it for her. This move, it was for Lucy, to go somewhere quieter, somewhere closer to the nature that calmed her. All this was on Lucy. She kept walking.

"Well. Goodnight then."

Lucy climbed up to her room again to her book, her comfort. It would be a while before she slept. She listened to the mumbled half-conversation until she heard the chair slide back on the kitchen tiles, and then turned off her bedroom light. Mum's feet were heavy on the stairs, despite the fluffy slipper socks. Her bedroom door clicked. Lucy lay awake.

At 2:36 a.m., Lucy woke with a start and looked at her clock. Her brain felt fuzzy and there was sleep dust in her eyes. She rubbed it away and decided to get up. A chapter of her book would hopefully get her off to sleep again. Her book had fallen out of her hand last night and tumbled under her bed where she couldn't quite reach it.

Her bedside light was still on, so she swung her feet out onto the cold floorboards. The light seemed far too bright for a moment, so she switched it off. Her room was completely silent, which was strange because usually there were little noises. Her brother snoring in the next room, the wind catching the panes and shifting them with a gentle knock, the radiator giving off an absent-minded 'tink tink' as the water negotiated its way around the airlocks. But there was nothing, just silent darkness.

Lucy picked up her book and put it on the little table next to her clock. Then she noticed a beam of light through a gap in her curtains. That wasn't right. She padded towards the window and pulled them aside. It was coming from the meadow. Eerie blue light danced like a silk scarf in the wind, flinging itself this way and that, and then back again, touching the tops of the trees and causing the leaves to change shape in its billowing shadows. Though the bushes were completely still, the twirling light made them seem frantic, like a thousand candles flickering in unison.

It was beautiful. Lucy had seen the Northern Lights on the TV, but they were nothing like this. At the same time, she felt like she must go outside. She had a strong urge to be among this strange light show. She padded to her bedroom door, opened it as quietly as she could and deftly made her way down the stairs to the front door. For some reason the creaky stair stayed quiet, as though she merely floated over it, weightless.

Through the kitchen and out of the back door towards the path. She was barefoot. How could that be? She could never be barefoot outside. She ascended the same path she now knew so well, towards the lights that were calling her. Each step brought her closer. The broccoli bushes stretched out their stubby branches, lengthening like fingers unfolding, offering their woody palms. The old, deep earth smell mixed with the newness of damp tree buds. She grasped a sapling to steady herself, strong like a leg bone but flexing under her effort.

The air tasted different now as she approached the meadow. Crisper and older. The path opened out and her feet met the soil, grass seeming to grow between her toes as she stepped, and a familiar but gentler tingling in her veins. Away from the cottage fumes of old mould and stale breakfast bacon. Away from the security of four walls. The Yew was beckoning, full facing her on the open hill. The lights danced on her bare arms and made them tingle.

Now she could see where the lights were from. Two figures stood under the boughs of the Yew, arms outstretched. One was a woman, one was a child. No wait, not a child: a small person, but definitely older. The shape was all wrong. Too thin. They were looking up into the branches, and the Yew's bark was swirling and whirling. Lucy walked towards them, pulled by the lights as if someone had grabbed the front of her pyjamas and was tugging her.

They were chanting in a strange guttural language that was beautiful and yet vicious. The words seemed urgent, getting faster and faster, repeating the same sounds over and over. The lights became more frantic, too, flashing past her face, darting around her. Her feet were drawn into the ground. The electricity was stronger now, flowing through her soles and into her calf muscles, up and into her spine and gripping at the back of her neck. She could feel the creatures beneath her, the beetles scuttling and worms stretching their way through their self-made tunnels, the spiders and earwigs scurrying to a million different destinations. She could feel they had a purpose. They were building, protecting, preparing the soil against danger. And then she felt the roots of the grass and the bushes, all connected. All flowing towards the Yew, pulsing in channels, teeming with energy.

Lucy gasped at the power she felt beneath her, inside her. Her fingers reached up, too, as the figures were doing, and her mouth uttered the same guttural words, flooding from her throat and up unto the still sky.

At that moment the woman turned. It was the woman from the fair. Her eyes flashed. She made a swift movement, brushing her right hand away over her shoulder and towards her. Lucy felt a rush of wind, and an invisible hand grabbed her and was pulling her roughly backwards through the air, leaving her arms and legs flailing out in front. She was flying at ground level, sucked back towards the cottage. Then blackness.

And then there was light, bright and warm. She was under her duvet, the sunlight was streaming through the gap in her curtains, her clock was beeping. 7:00 a.m. Her book was still on the floor where it fallen from her hands. Hadn't she picked that up? The sleep dust was back. She rubbed it away. Her brother was humming and clanking cups together, the kettle was boiling, and her Mum was rustling something in her room across the landing.

Lucy swung her legs out from bed and sat up. What a strange dream. Without thinking she got up and headed downstairs, forgetting her slippers and dressing gown, which she always put on without fail, every morning.

"Morning, Luce. Wanna cuppa?" Danny was leaning against the work surface. "You OK, Luce? You look like you've been having a fight with your duvet! Your hair is a sight to be seen!"

Mum came downstairs with a plastic crate full of washing. "Lucy look at your feet! What on earth have you been doing! They're filthy!"

Lucy opened her mouth to try and speak but couldn't find any words.

"Luce, where are your slippers? You never go barefoot!" Mum was staring at her.

Lucy didn't know what to say. It was true, she never went barefoot like this, but this morning it was OK. Her feet felt different, as though they'd been through some sort of transition. Was it true, then? Had she really ventured out into the meadow last night? Had she really seen that woman? And who was the other figure, too small to be human? Danny handed her a mug.

"I've put an extra sugar in it. Looks like you need it this morning!" She managed an uncertain smile at Danny and sipped at the steaming tea.

7

The Job

"It's just a couple of days, love, that's all. Danny will be here, and I'll get Grandma to come and visit to check on you. When I come back, we'll start on that Internet school stuff, OK?"

Lucy's throat had seized up. It wasn't that she needed her mum there all the time, it's just that it was different. She and Danny would do things differently. It would mean her brain would have to work things out, cope with unpredictability, eat different food! She tensed and closed her eyes. They'd only been there a few weeks. It was too soon.

"Look, Luce, I have to finish this off. It's my last London job, and if I don't complete it, I don't get the money. I've got the mortgage to pay."

Mum looked at her despairingly. Lucy knew all this. She knew Mum had to do this. She knew how the world worked for single parents, the constant juggle, working it out from one week to the next. Dad always paid his dues, but it was never enough. Not if you lived round here, anyway.

"I'll be back before you even realise I've gone. I'll get all your favourites in. I'll even get you M&Ms, one for each day. How's about that?"

Lucy nodded slowly, although she felt like her shoulders were still up around her ears. Danny handed her a bottle of milk. She looked at it, not processing why he'd given it to her.

"For your cornflakes, freakoid, the ones you just poured yourself?" He winked at her. Right. Yes. Cornflakes. She could do this. She just needed to take one day at a time. Mum wasn't going til next week. She'd have time to get used to it, time to plan. It would be OK. She poured the milk into her bowl. It had to be touching the bottom of the blue pattern around the edge. That would be the right amount. She always had this bowl for that reason, so she could tell it was right. If it went above that imaginary line, she would have to pour some out. She got it just right. She could do this. Lucy took a deep breath.

"OK, Mum."

"That's my girl." Mum smiled at her with relief. She let go of the breath she'd been holding in. It wafted and smelt of tea and toast, with a hint of toothpaste. She got up and put her mug in the sink. "You know, I got a letter from the council yesterday. We're officially registered as homeschooling! That'll be an adventure, won't it?" She wore a thin smile that meant she was actually terrified by the whole idea but was doing her best not to show it.

Lucy knew this wasn't what her mum wanted. After the last school had called yet another meeting, Mum had stalked out. She'd sworn at the head. It was quite impressive at the time. Lucy had had to trot after her out of the gates as Mum muttered under her breath. That was the last time Lucy went there—not that she'd been to many classes anyway.

The homeschooling thing was a last resort. Mum was clueless about where to start. The school had just been glad they weren't responsible anymore. Mum said it all boiled down to money at the end of the day. Money, money, money. Mortgages, bills, can't afford this, can't afford that. Lucy was so jealous of those rabbits in the meadow, happily bimbling among the buttercups, stuffing their furry muzzles with sweet grass. It was why Mum clung to all her posh clothes, bought when times were easier.

"You ready, Danny?" Mum put her hand on his shoulder.

"Ready as I'll ever be, I s'pose."

"OK, Luce, grab your coat. We need to get there by ten."

They were dropping Danny off at the Jobcentre in the nearest town twenty minutes away. Until he had his own transport, getting gigs was difficult in a rural area. In the meantime, it was whatever work he could get.

They climbed into the car and headed off. The day was grey. Sombre clouds blanketed the countryside and it was starting to drizzle. The bright lights of last night were forgotten, as though the meadow had dreamed it too, and had woken up oblivious to what had occurred.

After forty minutes, Danny dumped his bag in the footwell and got in. Everything about him seemed heavy. The clouds had darkened further, the drizzle had turned to persistent drops, and the windows of the car had steamed up. Lucy had been drawing flowers on the window and was the first to spy Danny coming through one of the petals. His eyebrows were furrowed, and his fringe was plastered against his forehead.

"So?"

"There's a cleaning job, evenings at a primary school. But by the time I pay the bus fare, I come back with pittance."

Danny slammed the car door.

"I've signed on, at least. Interview next Tuesday. I start getting money in a week."

Mum tried to give him a sympathetic look. Danny crossed his arms and turned to look out of his window.

"If I was in London, I'd be gigging."

"I know, Danny, I know." There wasn't much more Mum could say. She turned the ignition key, checked over her shoulder, and then pulled out of the lay-by they'd been waiting in. She let out a long sigh. "We'll get there, Danny, I promise. We'll get there somehow."

Nobody spoke on the way back. The puddles splashed up against the car and the windscreen wipers squeaked. Mum put the radio on quietly because she knew it set Lucy off, but it still irritated her. As they drove further away from the town the signal started to get weaker and the incessant beat of a rock song from ten years ago started to fizz in and out. Mum tutted and switched it off. Danny, who would normally be commenting on every song, giving its date of release and interesting facts about the history of the drummer or something, just stared out the window. The car smell was damp and cloying and Lucy's window flowers were slowly misting up again.

8

The Break

"It didn't work. We need the Council here."

They both shivered, despite the stove door being open. The glow was fierce, and the new logs crackled with damp.

"It was the girl. She saw everything."

"No, not her. She was giving us what she had to help, did you not see? She was speaking the old language."

"Then why did you send her back?"

Ceinwen placed another log in the stove. Its weight caused the others to shift and let out sparks onto the already singed mat. Ceinwen sat down, hunched forward and looking at the flames, said,

"For protection. I could feel the tree weakening. I didn't want her near. She's human."

"But how? How did she know?"

"I told you she was different. I told you she'd seen me at the fair."

Puck sat at the table as he had before, drained, tired. Ceinwen had sliced some dark brown bread, spread thick with butter. It sat, bloated, on a chipped plate with an apple and a hunk of cheese.

"Eat. You need to renew your strength." Ceinwen chewed on her own portion, the butter squeezing into the corner of her mouth. Crumbs skidded off her chin and onto her skirt.

"Thank you."

Puck took a bite from his bread. His mouth was dry, and the bread made him cough. He took a swig of the blackberry wine Ceinwen had poured for him without asking if he wanted any.

Ceinwen swallowed. "We have to try again tonight. The risk is too great not to. The tree is weakening, I can feel it."

Puck felt it, too. He would need strength to perform the rites again tonight, and despite a lengthy meeting, the Council had refused to acknowledge a problem. The barriers were weak; it would take one event for Gwyllgi to break through, and with his followers streaming behind him, there would be nothing to stop him ravaging the countryside. He remembered the last time well enough. It was what started the first great war. Feeding on greed, anger, bigotry, Gwyllgi had made the whole world hate each other, whispering in the ears of humans who knew no better, urging them to destroy, his shadow merging with theirs, using his influence and then gleeful in watching the humans pitted against each other. They'd managed to contain him, eventually, but it had taken the entire might of the Council several weeks. That was once they'd found him, of course.

Puck bit into the apple.

"Ugh, a maggot." He watched it curl out of the hole he'd made, flinging itself this way and that, suddenly unprotected by the flesh.

"Mine, too." Ceinwen held up the one from her plate. "This is bad. These were from the apple tree by the gate. It's the Sentinel for the cottage, my home. It's what keeps it undetected, and it's never been ruptured. The building will be visible soon."

Ceinwen looked grimly at her plate, no longer hungry. The bread looked dusty, the cheese pale and dry.

"I've been here since 1914. More than a hundred years I've guarded this prison. A century of keeping my promise never to leave, always alone. I've kept my vow, and I've done my duty, but I'm old."

She looked at her hands, palms up, rough skin on the pads, brown score lines and bulging knuckles. Her ring, a solid heavy brass, sat stalwart on her finger. She'd not removed it since it was placed there during the binding ceremony. She'd worked so hard for so long, placing these hands on the Yew, letting it collect her magic, a little every day, to keep it strong. What had she done to let it fail now?

"I've given this place my life. Now this."

Puck had not seen her like this. She was always Ceinwen. Tough, rugged, stable. To see her doubt herself was agonising. This figure of strength was hunched in her chair, looking frail and small. This couldn't be right, couldn't be happening. He laid his hand on hers.

"Tonight, we will try again." She glanced at his fist, small against her own. "And I'll attempt to summon the Council."

9

The Trip

Lucy stood with her shoulder on the door frame, watching Danny as he put a small wheelie suitcase in the boot of Mum's car. She fussed with it, slammed the boot shut, then put her handbag on the front passenger seat, checking she had her phone for the thousandth time. Pink petals edged with brown had collected on the roof from the elderly cherry tree in the driveway, and she brushed them off impatiently. Ducking under an ancient bough, she trudged around to the driver's door and clicked the handle.

"OK, so your Nan is coming late morning tomorrow. She'll get a taxi from the station, so make sure you're in when she arrives. She's staying one night, so you'll need to call her another taxi on Wednesday morning, OK?"

Danny nodded, then winked at Lucy. She'd repeated this same information three times in the last half hour.

"We'll be all right, Mum." He gave her a thin smile and rattled some coins in his pocket. "It's not like I'm going anywhere, is it?"

Mum sighed. "Not now, Danny. We'll talk when I get back." She looked tired. There were circles under her eyes, and she'd lost weight. Her favourite work top hung loose around her hips and Lucy could see her collar bones protruding from under her scarf. A petal had stuck to her hair, and it got into the car with her as if wanting to go on an adventure of its own. Lucy went to the kitchen. She heard a mumbled goodbye and then the car engine fired and tyres crunched gravel. She'd gone. Lucy hugged herself tight and paced the kitchen. Three times around the table, then three times back. Then she went upstairs and sat on her bed. Humming, she opened her book to where she'd stopped reading at 4:00 a.m. this morning and tried to focus on the words.

Danny's trainers scuffed up the stairs and he knocked lightly on her door.

"All right, Mucka?" He had a grey hoodie on, and jeans that had rips at the knees. His hair still had the tufts that always stuck up for at least two hours after he'd got out of bed, and he needed a shave. Lucy opened her mouth, but nothing happened. Her words had stuck in her throat again. She'd read the same paragraph three times and had still not taken it in, so she closed her book and put it back on her bedside table. She looked at his chin.

"Hang on… I know what'll do the trick." Danny's eyes twinkled and he disappeared into his room. He came back holding his oldest and most favourite guitar and plonked himself down next to her on the bed. The mattress rocked and Lucy felt her stomach lurch.

"Right then, you know the one…four bars intro and I'll sing the descant."

He started picking at the strings, his rough fingers sliding over the frets and making them yelp softly between each chord. He paused expectantly on the fourth change, and when nothing happened, he played the same again.

"Don't leave me hanging, sis!"

This made Lucy break into a smile and the weight lifted from her chest. She rolled her eyes teasingly. "Oh, all right then."

The fourth chord rang, anticipating the first word of a song that they had been singing together for years. It was one of Danny's, one he'd made up once after a bad day when Lucy's words had left her completely, and when only Danny had been able to coax her out of a cupboard. He'd sat cross legged on the kitchen floor that day, strumming lightly and making up silly song words.

The sausages are yellow and the ketchup's running blue,

The frying pan is freezing and the cat is in the loo,

The bananas in the fruit bowl have decided on a waltz,

And the carpet in the living room has upped and gone to France!

Ohhhhh,

the carpet in the living room has upped and gone to France!

We have an old umbrella that has journeyed to the moon,

And the Wellingtons will miss him if he doesn't come back soon,

The books in Lucy's bedroom have decided to escape,

And the curtains in the bathroom have just stolen all the soap

Aaaand,

The curtains in the bathroom have just stolen all the soap!

Danny ended with a dramatic strum, raising his arm in the air and nodding to an imaginary crowd.

"Thanks, everyone, thank you so much, and to all my fans…goodnight!" He closed his eyes, stood up and did a full-length bow to Lucy's teddy bear, who was staring blankly from her pillow.

Lucy giggled and Danny grinned at her. "That's better. That's my Lucy. I can't believe you keep that voice just for me. You're still amazing, you know."

Lucy looked at her knees. She had only ever managed to sing in front of Danny. It was their thing.

"And now for lunch… Cheese and ham toastie suit you, Madam? It's my specialty…"

Lucy nodded. She took a deep breath, smoothed her hands on her jeans, and stood up. It was going to be OK.

They could do this together. They could make a life here. Danny would get a job, Mum would finally be happy, and she could live. Just live.

10

The Phone Call

That evening they sat eating freezer pizza on the sofa, laughing through an old DVD that jumped occasionally as the player tried to cope with the scratches. Danny had his feet up on the coffee table, which Mum usually told him off for, and Lucy had a heavy blanket over her knees, which felt so good. The weight of it folded over her legs and hung through to the seat cushion, hugging her skin and letting her sink into the sofa cushion.

It was one of those old-looking ones with square woven patterns. They'd found it in a cupboard upstairs, and it had become Lucy's immediately. Her feet were bare and free, and she wriggled her toes through the fibres of the carpet. They felt weird. It was so unusual for her to have bare feet, anywhere, even in the house, but for some reason, since that night in the meadow, she just needed her feet to have contact with the floor whenever possible. She pressed her soles into the rough wool and enjoyed the itchy strands pushing back.

The afternoon had been great. Danny had played guitar while Lucy sang along. Silly songs, songs from his old band, a couple of oldies from Mum's car CD. He'd got in three massive bags of M&Ms and they had spent fifteen minutes sorting them into colours, Danny scoffing the red ones because he said they were probably evil and needed to be dispatched immediately. The green ones were in a bag on Lucy's lap. She pinched one carefully out and placed it in the front of her mouth, letting the sugar melt on her tongue. When all the outer surface had gone, and only the thin white layer remained, she bit through and let the chocolate swim around her cheeks.

Then Danny's phone rang. His ring tone was a guitar solo from some 80s rock band, and it sang out, cutting through the room, spectacular and intrusive.

Danny sighed and said, "Ros."

"Do you want me to pause the film?"

"S'OK, I've seen it a million times. I'll go outside."

He answered with an apprehensive 'hello' and then got up off the sofa, heading out into the garden. Lucy's blanket slipped and she grabbed it, pulling it up over her arms. It let out a musty draught.

Danny had left the front door ajar and she could hear a muffled conversation.

"No, I can't, you know that...Lucy...I don't have the money yet...But Ros, you know...Ros, listen..."

Lucy got up and peeked through the living room curtain. He was under the cherry, fingers combing through his fringe, kicking at the fallen petals which were mulching themselves to the gravel.

His voice was getting louder and he started waving his arms. He paced this way and that. Then he flung his phone on the ground and sank down with his back on the trunk. His hands covered his face and his shoulders were shuddering. Lucy bounced on her toes and started humming. She hated seeing Danny like this. She felt what he felt, just from looking at him. She started breathing deeply. In, out, in, out. She felt the air pushing deep onto her diaphragm. It was OK, he would be OK, she told herself.

Danny got up and called through the door. "I need ten minutes, Luce, OK?" His voice cracked. "I'll be up on the meadow. Just ten minutes OK?"

"OK."

"Keep watching the film. I won't be long."

"Erm, OK."

Danny closed the door and she heard his feet crunch the gravel, getting quieter as he made his way around the side of the house.

Lucy sat down on the sofa again and looked at her watch. 8:47 p.m. OK, so he'd be back at 8:57. He'd always said that she needed to add five minutes to that, in case he was delayed. But he would always be coming back. Like if Mum had gone in the petrol station to pay, and there was a queue, and Lucy had stayed in the car as it was quieter. Or like if he'd gone to post a letter, or get some milk from the corner shop back in London, and Lucy had stayed at the house. So 9:02, then.

She slipped the pack of Post-it Notes and pen out of her back pocket and wrote:

8:57

so she wouldn't forget, then held them with both hands, flicking the corner with her thumb.

Lucy watched the TV screen. It was the scene when the two heroes had ventured into a cave, thinking it was safe, but their enemy had been hiding in it, so they had to fight. Swords clashed and dramatic orchestra music trilled. Lucy loved how the camera angles changed more rapidly to make it seem more exciting.

8:53 p.m. Lucy patted the blanket around her knees. She ate three more M&Ms, letting them melt, rolling them around with her tongue. The sword fight ended, the enemy was defeated and was left pleading on his knees.

Nine o'clock. This was OK. It was within the five minutes 'just in case' time. Lucy paused the film and listened. The characters froze comically, one with eyes closed and a word poised on his lips. Silence. No footsteps on the gravel. The room had darkened. The spring sun had dipped below the horizon and the remains of the dusk had given up stretching its fingers across the sky and had let go, allowing the night to smother the garden.

9:08. Lucy got up and looked through the curtains, expecting Danny to be jogging around the house, just about to unlock the door and apologise breathily for taking longer than the time he had said. He knew she needed it to be exact. He knew she had to know when. She hefted the blanket around her shoulders, bouncing her toes and humming quietly.

Nothing. Something was wrong. She still held the Post-it notepad with the time on it. Had she written it down wrong? She traced the number with her finger. No, he'd definitely said ten minutes.

9:14. Lucy jogged up to her room and flung her curtains aside. Come on, Danny, walk down the path. She silently urged him to appear. The lump in her chest was growing now. She bounced her toes again and balled her fists, willing herself not to jump and flap as her body wanted her to. Deep breaths, in, out, in, out.

9:17

9:20

Something was definitely wrong.

Then there was a flash. The garden was suddenly daylight. Blinded, Lucy covered her eyes for a moment, the back of her head fizzing with electricity. Then just as quickly, there was blackness.

11

The Taking

Lucy held her breath. Nothing happened. The light was there, and then not. It was definitely coming from the meadow, though.

In that moment she made the bravest decision of her life, in a split second, with only one thought: Danny.

Running down the stairs she flung open the back door, and without even bothering to cover her feet she fled towards the path, blanket scraping and bumping behind her. The way was surprisingly easy without shoes and her toes curled around roots and stones as if they knew the way themselves. Out onto the meadow and the soles of her feet immediately recognised that same tingling she had felt before. Lucy gasped. She could feel every creature, every creeping root from the bushes and trees, every particle of soil around her. It was as if her pulse matched theirs and they were calling to her in unison. She hadn't been to the meadow since that night, too frightened to discover if it was all true after all.

There was no time to wonder. She headed straight for the Yew. Three figures were black against the dark purple sky, pin-pricked with stars. She recognised one as Danny, the other two, the child, no, the small man and the old lady; they were shouting at Danny to *STOP!* Danny was walking away, over the brow.

Lucy broke into a run. Her calf muscles strained as she pushed them as hard as she could up the slope and towards her brother.

"DANNY!" she yelled, her voice aching with the volume. The old woman spun round to see her.

"DANNY! WAIT!"

But he couldn't hear her. He was drawn to something she couldn't see. The small man, who had been holding his hands high, eyes blazing and back spasming, was flung back onto the grass. Then Lucy noticed the old woman was clutching her arm to her chest, the wrist at a strange angle. A trickle of a memory. The day at the fair. Could it be?

"DANNY!"

She was almost there, she could see the old woman's hair, frantic in the night air, and the small man sprawled in the grass, too thin to be a child, his features older and yet free from any signs of age. The moment she reached the brow she saw Danny walking steadily forward, his hands outspread and his face up towards…

…towards the most magnificent, terrifying creature.

"Stop! Or he'll take you, too."

The woman's good hand held firm on Lucy's arm, her eyes piercing into her, warning her of the danger. Lucy could feel her nails digging into her skin, unyielding.

The creature's eyes blazed red. It was a large dog, bigger than a shire horse, with matted black fur. Its muzzle dripped with spit, and two yellow fangs protruded, spearing into its bloodied fur. The legs were half bone, excess flesh peeling and mixing with the pelt, claws digging deep into the soil, as though paring back the meadow's skin. The creature snarled, and inside its mouth burned with a green flame, tongue lashing, tasting the air as though readying itself to gulp the whole night down into its gullet.

Danny was still walking towards it, pulled by an unseen force, gazing into the creature's eyes. His face was white, his eyes fixed.

"DANNY!"

Lucy ripped her arm away from the woman and let the blanket fall to the ground, running.

"NO!"

The small man had leaped up and in a deft movement flung the blanket over Lucy, holding it tight around her.

"You must keep this around you." His voice was urgent in her ear. "He will be taken. We cannot stop it now, but you cannot help him if you are taken, too."

Lucy sank to the ground, knees in the damp grass, her fingers pushing into the soil for comfort. The man was gripping her shoulders, holding her down. The insects beneath her were buzzing. They were telling her to hold still, hang back, wait. They seemed to pull her palms into the ground, gluing her fingers to the loam.

The creature raised his paw, scissor-like claws clicking as he raised them to Danny's chest. Another blinding flash, and they were gone. Lucy wept and cried aloud into the night.

12

The Blanket

Red-eyed and sore cheeked, Lucy sat in a tatty armchair in a cottage that hadn't existed an hour ago. At least, she hadn't been able to see it, as the old woman had explained. Puck, as was his name, was bandaging her wrist as best he could. Ceinwen had told him of a jar in the kitchen which contained some potent-smelling dried moss, which he was now weaving in with strips of cotton cloth, chanting strange sounding yet slightly familiar words under his breath. Lucy knew the name from fairy stories, and from when she'd been sent out of class again last September and had absent-mindedly picked up *The Complete Works of Shakespeare* from the library shelf. It was a strange name for a grown-up, even one of his stature. To be named after a fairy. He didn't seem the type.

"Damn lucky you had that blanket with you, girl." The woman's voice was gruff but kind. She winced as Puck ripped the end of a strip in two and knotted them around her wrist to secure it.

"Surely you need a hospital for that?" Lucy sipped at some murky-looking tea which had been handed to her very shortly after her arrival and had made her feel better immediately. Her feet were still bare, and she could feel the edges of the floorboards through the thin rug. She surprised herself by being able to speak at all after what had happened. Strange as this cottage and these two characters were, she just knew in her gut that they were the right people to be with right now. In any other part of her life, the shock of so much unknown, of all the unexpected newness, would have sent her running. The tea itself was nothing like she'd ever tasted before. Both fresh and bitter, with a sweetness that lingered on her tongue long after she swallowed.

"And what would I tell them? Eh? I'm over a hundred and fifty years old and your brother broke my wrist and then popped off on holiday with a giant dog?" She chuckled, but it was not a happy sound.

"Be gentle with her, Ceinwen. This is all new to her." Puck, having finished bandaging, sat heavily onto a dining chair.

"You're a hundred and fifty years old?!"

"Give or take a few years. Can't quite remember. Birthdays weren't counted so precisely where I came from."

"And what did you say about my brother?"

Ceinwen sighed. Puck placed his hand on Lucy's shoulder. "I think we need to tell you from the beginning," he said, "starting with why that blanket just saved you from being taken by one of the most powerful magical creatures in the world."

Lucy pulled the old blanket tighter around her shoulders. It still had the same musty smell it'd had before, and the wool itched slightly against the bare skin on her wrists. The heavy folds draped across her lap like an old sheepdog, seeming to breathe gently as though asleep. She'd just found it in a cupboard in her room on moving in day. Mum had assumed it had been left by the previous owners, given it one sniff and passed it to Lucy, saying she could do what she liked with it. She traced the patterns with her finger. The background was a moss green on one side, cream and black on the other. The blocks of colour were different on each side and looked a bit like the waffles she'd had in a cafe once. Uniform lines of woven thread made speckles as they square-danced with each other.

"That, my girl, is a proper antique Welsh blanket. Made in the Teifi Valley in the Caenarfon pattern, if I remember rightly. The essence of every generation that has used that blanket to keep them warm has woven itself through the fibres. The older a blanket is, the more protection it will give you, and a tiny bit of your magic will remain in it for future generations, too. You were drawn to it, yes?"

Lucy nodded. It was true that as soon as she had touched it, it had felt like hers. Mum had thought she was crazy at the time, wanting a smelly old blanket so much.

"Not many can sense it, but you obviously can. In fact, I think it's been proven you can sense a lot more than most."

"But why would it protect me from that…thing?"

"Love." Ceinwen paused and sat back in her chair, wincing with the pain in her wrist. "Love, pure and simple. Blankets like that were usually made for gifts. Wedding presents, anniversaries. They were placed on children when they were sleeping to keep out a bitter winter. They were treasured and looked after carefully because of what they represented: safety and family. Things that creature abhors."

Lucy looked at the blanket with new eyes and placed the palm of her hand gently on a fold. Just as in the meadow when she had felt the creatures in the soil through the soles of her feet, she now sensed a distant, warm sound of chattering through the tips of her fingers. An old song in a strange tongue sung around a fire. Families stretching back a hundred years. It made her smile, despite everything that had happened that evening.

"What's it doing here? This isn't Wales."

"I could ask the same about myself." Ceinwen chuckled wryly, but her eyes were watery. "It wasn't that long ago that everyone spoke the old language. What was Welsh and what wasn't Welsh wasn't considered important. The world is much older than you think"

"So what's that about my brother breaking your arm? He wouldn't do that, he's the most gentle person in the world." Lucy felt suddenly very defensive and balled her fists. The tea was having a strange effect on her. She shook her head to remember just how she'd felt in the meadow. Why was everyone so calm? Why were they just sitting around when her brother had gone? The anger and terror were still there, but wrapped up in something, muted inside her. It was a bizarre sensation to know it was there, yet not feel it fully.

"It's OK, it wasn't deliberate. He broke a Yew bough. Ceinwen and that tree are, shall we say, linked?" Puck glanced at Ceinwen for permission to continue.

"Carry on, Sprite. I'm interested in your version of events." She looked at Lucy intently and watched as she struggled with her own emotions, not wanting to 'switch them on' again, but at the same time feeling weird that they weren't there. It was showing on Lucy's face. "It's OK, Lucy, it's the tea. Your emotions will return. Don't worry."

Lucy let go, let the effects of the tea wash over her. For some reason, she trusted this strange woman. There was something about her. Something familiar, as though she was family. A distant cousin she'd never met. But that was ridiculous. Lucy shook away the thought.

"Tell me," she said.

"OK, so, as you are now aware, there are some magical creatures that exist in this world that you may not previously have realised." Puck sighed deeply. "Some of them are less than helpful to the human population."

"Evil," Ceinwen blurted. "They're evil, Puck. Don't try and soften it for the girl."

"OK, so yes, Ceinwen is right, they are evil, and they encourage evil thoughts in humans. Greed, bigotry, anger, hate. Over the centuries this has led to wars, famine, disasters."

"So that huge dog thing was one of them, right?" Lucy's bare feet felt cold. She shivered and shrugged the blanket a little closer.

"He is Gwyllgi, Dire Wolf, Dog of Darkness, Black Hound, whatever name you wish for him. He's one of the oldest and most powerful, and we thought we had contained him here."

"What do you mean, 'here'? What is this place?"

"Well, this meadow is not what it seems to the human eye. It is a place we have worked hard to keep secure over many years. To keep the less savoury characters away from where they can cause trouble."

"Do you mean it's a prison?" Lucy couldn't really believe that this beautiful green space could contain any evil at all.

"In a way, yes. It is a kind of doorway that we keep locked. They are here, but not here. Do you understand?"

"I think so. But what has the Yew and my brother got to do with it?"

"Well, did you know that trees have a tremendous power to talk to each other and send messages through the ground?"

Lucy shook her head.

"They do. They use the tiny creatures and plants in the earth to send messages. That Yew is the Sentinel for this meadow, just as the Apple Tree is the Sentinel for Ceinwen's cottage, and the Cherry is the Sentinel for your place down the hill. The Yew, with a little help from us, has been keeping that doorway closed for a very long time.

Ceinwen has been looking after it and topping it up to make sure it has enough strength. Unfortunately, there are a few things that can open the doorway. Human anger aimed at a Sentinel is one of them. Your brother broke a branch, but there must have been so much anger in his heart that it ripped open the barrier and let Gwyllgi through. The barriers have been weaker lately, as the tree ages—"

"And me," Ceinwen added. "I haven't got much left to give." Her resolved expression softened. Puck reached out his hand to hers.

"You are still the most powerful human I know, Ceinwen. These are dark days. Even the Council knows their magic needs to increase to keep things in order."

Ceinwen scoffed. Her jaw became set again. "They're not here though, are they?" After a moment she nodded for Puck to continue.

"As I was saying, the trees guard the entrances, but they also serve as protection for places of importance. The Apple helps this cottage remain unseen. Or it did."

"So why does our house have a Sentinel?"

"We're not really sure. That building is one of the oldest in this area, built at the same time as the Inn, and your Cherry has been there ever since we can remember. It's likely that someone lived there many years ago who knew about the non-human world and was trying to protect it. It could be linked to that blanket. Who knows?"

Lucy remembered the petal that had stuck to Mum's hair as she drove away. Maybe it was trying to tell her something.

Ceinwen shuffled in her chair, trying to make her wrist more comfortable. "They call them 'pubs' now, Puck. Showing your age there." She chuckled wryly. "You see, humans remember their history through writing it down, but if the non-human world did that there is a risk they would be discovered. We use stories, but if the last person who knows that story dies, then the history dies with them. There's many a mystery in these parts that will never be solved. The information is lost now." She reached forward to touch the blanket. The tip of her finger on a fold, Lucy could see that Ceinwen felt what she did. "It was an old family."

There was something that Ceinwen wasn't saying. There was a secret that was being kept. She knew more about that cottage but wasn't saying it. There were grey folds by her eyes that held memories of something long gone.

"Maybe they lived here because they knew the meadow was special?" Lucy asked.

"Or maybe the meadow is special because of that family." She was wistful for a moment, but then the look was gone. "The magic has always been strong here. It's why it was chosen."

Puck stood up, took Lucy's now empty mug, and started swilling it in the sink. "The question now is how do we get Gwyllgi to release your brother? What's his name, did you say?"

"Danny." The word stuck in Lucy's throat and tears started to gather in the corners of her eyes again. She felt her cheeks flushing. She knew why Danny had done it. He was angry, he felt rejected and trapped, but he didn't want to show that in front of her. He'd gone to the meadow to try and get rid of the black in his heart before returning to her. This was all her fault. All Danny wanted to do was protect her like he always had. She rucked the rug with her toes and started to rock in the chair. Her emotions were squirming. Even the tea couldn't hold them back.

"You need to move." Ceinwen looked at her with an intense stare that seemed to lay Lucy bare, like an open book, her life story there to be read in an instant. "You're like me. You need to move, and you need to be outside."

Lucy nodded, surprised that this old woman, whom she had known for so little time, knew her like a sister. There was an undeniable connection with her. An older soul, but a similar one. She could see how the way Ceinwen spoke would be taken as forthright, rude almost, but that she didn't mean it. She spoke the truth, whether others wanted to hear or not, and Lucy liked that.

They ventured outside. The night air was bitter and it stung Lucy's cheeks, but it was good to be in the open. She breathed it in, and the inside of her throat became icy cold. It was a calming feeling. Her bare feet were planted firmly on the ground. She could sense everything she had before, but this time she had more control. It wasn't in charge of her anymore. It seemed as if the creatures were waiting, just beneath, for her to tell them what to do. It felt powerful, and her back straightened. Her head was high, and she imagined she was as tall as the Yew beside her as her skin fizzed pleasantly.

"Feels good, yes?" Ceinwen stood next to her, looking out over the meadow.

"Yes," Lucy answered breathily, "but I don't know what to do. My Mum's away on a work trip and Danny's disappeared. What will I tell her?"

Ceinwen looked away and contemplated for a moment. "It is difficult to have to lie to someone you love, but that is what you shall need to do. Tell your mother what happened, that your brother became angry and left the house, but omit the events in the meadow. Say you waited and then called her."

"And then what? Where is he? How do we get him back?" Lucy's throat tightened again. "I have to see him. I can't be without him. He helps me so much. You don't understand!" Lucy hugged the blanket around herself as hard as she could, feeling her muscles tense against the wool. She needed Danny.

"Actually, I do. There was someone, once, a lifetime ago, who saved me from myself." Ceinwen's face softened just a little, then became closed again. Clearing her throat, she turned to Lucy. "Anyway, we shall get your brother back, but it will take time. You will need to manage things at home. Can you do that?"

Lucy nodded grimly. It would be down to her. Mum would be distraught, but there was no way she could tell her what really happened. There would be police to be called. She would have to put on an act. She would be protecting her mum, but also protecting a world she had just found. And anyway, who would believe her? Ceinwen was right. Lucy found herself humming softly. One note. Continuous. In anticipation of what was inevitable. Her skin tingled a little more.

"I will send you a message. Only you will know who it is from. When you get it, come as soon as you can. And bring that blanket."

Ceinwen strode away from the cottage over the brow of the hill without a goodbye. From the outside it was tumbled-down and weed-covered. The Apple tree hugged one wall, its limbs creeping around the stonework. There were patches in the bark and some of the branches had withered. Apples had fallen haphazardly, but the tree still fruited. Strange. This was the wrong time for apples. Lucy shrugged, reminding herself that apples at the wrong time of year was probably one of the least strange things she had discovered in the last couple of hours.

Turning to the Yew, she looked up into its limbs. The trunk was huge and straight, gnarled and twisting slightly as it rose. It swayed gently and creaked, its needle-like leaves brushing together in whispering conversation. She saw the offending break a short way up, around head height. Sap dribbled from the crack and the inner wood gaped yellow against its snake-like skin. It was only a small bough, but it lolled downwards in such a melancholy way. Lucy felt her wrist ache as though a wound had been there but was now healed. A scar that was just a memory. She thought of Ceinwen and her connection.

She turned and headed down the hill. There was such an urgency in her chest to find and rescue Danny, but there was nothing she could do. Not yet anyway. She would play her part, as Ceinwen had told her. She had never felt so much emotion inside her, but at the same time felt so controlled. Something had changed. Maybe it was the tea, but Lucy felt...different.

Once through the back door she padded through to the kitchen to find the ancient Bakelite house phone. She could recite both Mum's and Danny's mobile numbers off by heart. Taking a deep breath, she picked up the receiver, and dialled.

13

The Wait

Mum had rushed back from London, spending a fortune on a taxi to get to the station where her car was parked and then weaving at speed through the unlit lanes. She burst in, breathless, at 2:00 a.m.

"Lucy! Lucy, where are you?"

Lucy got up from the sofa where she had been calmly waiting and headed out to the hall.

"I'm here."

Her mum squeezed her in a tight hug, which she would normally have fought, but she knew Mum needed this. She could hear her heart beating hard in her chest and the faint smell of sweat under her perfume. She couldn't help but stiffen in the embrace.

"Are you OK, Lucy? Are you hurt? Did you stay in the house like I said? Has he come back? I cannot believe he left you. BOY, is he in trouble!"

Lucy wasn't sure which question to answer first. Suddenly, she had an overwhelming urge to cry, to let out the events of the night, and in relief that someone was there with her now. She felt the heat in her eyes all at once.

"Oh, Lucy, it's OK. I'm here now. I called the police on the way, but they said to wait until tomorrow." Mum let out a sob too. "This is so unlike him. I'm so worried."

Lucy led her to the sofa and they sat close to each other, something that hadn't happened since she was a toddler. It was uncomfortable. Lucy's skin stung with the touch, but Mum needed this, too. Lucy breathed deep and sniffed. She needed to play the part now.

"It's OK, Mum, I'm sure he'll come back. He broke up with Ros. He was just really angry."

"I know, love, I rang Ros and she said they'd had an argument. She said she hadn't seen him. I just hope to God he turns up there. I've told her to call me if he does. I never liked that girl."

Lucy said nothing. She didn't like Ros either, but part of her hoped he would turn up at her house and that everything she saw in the meadow had just been a dream.

"I picked up his phone from the garden, Mum. The screen's smashed." Mum took it and tried the power button. Nothing.

Mum placed it on the windowsill by the front door. "I tried to ring it a few times. You know, just in case."

"I'll go and put the kettle on, Mum. Let's watch some telly til tomorrow. There's nothing we can do until the police get here."

Mum looked at her in surprise, seeing unexpected maturity. "Erm, OK, love. Do you know how?"

"Yeah, Danny taught me. Do you want an M&M? I saved the blue ones."

Lucy walked to the kitchen and fetched two mugs from the cupboard, filling the kettle as Danny had taught her, and putting a tea bag in each mug. She padded to the fridge and retrieved the half bottle of milk and waited for the kettle to click. The steam danced and the kettle wriggled on its stand, and at the performance finale, the red lever at the base clicked upwards and it settled, hissing.

Lucy poured water on the teabags. Looking at her watch, she waited for exactly three minutes. Once she had fished out the teabags with a teaspoon and put them in the sink, she poured a centimetre of milk in each, lining it up so that it was two centimetres from the top. She smiled to herself, proud that she had remembered everything. Carefully, she took the two cups through and placed one on a mat on the coffee table.

"Wow, thanks, love. I didn't know you could do that." Mum looked tired and her eyes were red. Lucy picked up the bag of M&Ms and offered them.

"There's no green ones left. I ate them."

"That's OK, blues are my favourite." Mum took one and there were a few minutes of silence. They were both thinking the same thing. There was nothing they could do til tomorrow, but there was also no way they could sleep.

"DVD?"

"OK, Mum. Let's do that."

So there they sat. Next to each other, but not touching. Watching a scratched DVD that Lucy chose, but thought Mum would like. Waiting for the time to pass when they could do something. Silently frustrated.

Meanwhile, the night drew on til morning. The moon shone through a bare patch in the living room curtains and mixed with the yellow glow from the table lamp on the sideboard. There was little sound apart from the voices on the TV and the occasional rustling of the M&M bag, but only from Lucy. Mum's eyes were on the screen, but she wasn't watching it. Lucy knew because she wasn't reacting. To anything. She just sat and stared like her body was just a shell, and her mind was elsewhere. Mum was in there somewhere, but she'd shut down. Lucy looked at her, tracing with her eyes the lock of hair that was tucked behind her ear, just like Lucy did. Danny had her nose.

Lucy had always thought it was just her that needed to escape from the world sometimes. Her mum needed it, too. She just did it in a different way.

14

The Report

"Well, he's a nineteen-year-old lad with a chip on his shoulder. I'm sure he'll be back soon with his tail between his legs. In the meantime, I'll send out his description and we'll keep a look out."

Lucy imagined a greasy chip with ketchup dripping on the police officer's shoulder, and a tail, wagging and fluffy, protruding out from behind the dining chair he was perched on. He was the kind of person who spoke in riddles. 'Gone off on walkabout.' 'Left his post, did he?' 'I'm sure you've been out of your mind with worry, Madam.' 'What a beautiful little princess you have here…'

She was certainly not royalty, her brother was not a soldier, nor did he carry letters around, and Mum's brain was definitely still resting inside her skull, not outside. Lucy decided to keep quiet. Some people were just like that. Talking in similes and sayings, never what they actually meant.

Mum was being ultra-polite, but Lucy could see the frustration in her face. It was quite clear the police weren't going to do anything, at least until a couple of days had gone by. The officer took the photo Mum kept in her purse and folded his notebook over it.

"Right then, Madam, let us know if he comes back, or if you have any further information about the lad's whereabouts." He stood up, replaced his hat on his head from under his arm, and offered Mum his hand. Mum didn't see it as she was blowing her nose in a ragged tissue, so he wiped it awkwardly on his trousers and headed to the front door. "Erm, I'll let meself out, love, don't worry." The latch clicked, and his shiny boots crunched along the path until a car door slammed.

Mum sat heavily back on the sofa. "Well, he was bloody useless."

She picked out the last blue M&M from a bowl on the coffee table and crunched it slowly. "What do we do now, Luce?"

"I suppose we wait and see." Lucy wasn't used to being the one giving an answer to this sort of question. There was silence for a few minutes, or at least a quieter bit that only had Mum's sighing and the creak of her shoe as she wriggled her toes against the leather. "Erm. I'm hungry. Danny taught me how to make a ham sandwich. I'll make one for you if you like?"

Mum didn't answer. She was staring at a small stain on the living room carpet. She hadn't heard.

"I'll…I'll go and make a sandwich." Lucy padded to the kitchen again with the blanket still wrapped around her, this time to the bread bin. It was going to be a difficult day. There was nothing she could do until Ceinwen made contact, and she couldn't tell her mum the truth. She'd have to hold it all in, all this information she was storing in her brain. She couldn't tell, and couldn't do anything. She felt her heart beating against her chest and a big ball of worry was growing in her stomach. Lucy took a deep breath and opened the fridge. It was her turn to look after Mum for a change.

As she closed the door, milk bottles clinking and a packet of cheese shifting its weight in the highest compartment, she glanced out of the kitchen window. To her surprise she saw a face. Except it was just that. A face. Floating in mid-air, just outside of the glass. Lucy shrieked and dropped the packet of ham she was holding. It slapped to the floor tiles.

"You OK, Lucy?" Mum called thinly from the other room.

It was Ceinwen, she realised. She was just a blurry image, like she was made of fog. This must be the 'message' she'd spoken of.

"Fine, Mum. Sorry, the ham slipped out of my hand. The packet is wet." Although her hand was shaking, she managed not to convey her initial terror through her voice. Got to keep calm. Got to keep this from Mum.

The mist-face dispersed, drifting away to the side, for an instant leaving just part of a face with crevasses that wafted and rolled. It was gone. Lucy was left staring at the garden. The morning frost was melting, and the sunlight sparkled on the grass. It all looked so green. So fresh it was magical. Spring. Growth. Lucy felt a slight vibration to the air around her, as if it was there all along, but she'd only just been told to focus on it. Now it was obvious, and the soles of her feet started to itch slightly.

She picked up the pack of ham from the floor. She was going to have to work out how to get out of the house and up into the meadow. Lucy really was bad at lying. It just felt so wrong to state things that weren't a fact. The morning had taken all her energy, saying things and not saying others. Keeping her mum 'in the dark'. It caused an actual pain in the pit of her stomach. It was best to keep to as much of the truth as was possible. Maybe just keep in the things she couldn't say. So much was assumed about what she thought already, it wouldn't be too hard. She hoped.

She buttered two slices of bread, laid two slivers of ham on one side, placed the other bread slice on the top and then cut the sandwich in half. All in twos. It was satisfying when things matched like that. When Danny had first taught her, she'd wanted to make another one straight away, and Danny had said OK, but that he couldn't eat ten rounds of ham sandwiches, so maybe they could stick to three for now. Lucy smiled at the memory.

She put the sandwich on a small plate and carried it through to her mum.

"Not having one yourself, Luce?"

"No, I'm not really hungry yet."

Stick with the truth, stick with the truth, stick with the truth…

"Actually, Mum, I'm not feeling great. I'm just going to go to the meadow. Is that OK?"

Mum looked at her. The bit between her eyebrows was wrinkled. That meant she was worried.

"I won't go far. Promise."

"OK, love. I'll stay by the phone, but I want you back in half an hour, and you won't leave the meadow, OK? Promise?"

"Promise."

Lucy ran upstairs, ripped off her pyjamas and flung on jeans, t-shirt and socks as quickly as she could. She threw the blanket over her shoulders again. It still felt warm from her own body heat. Shoving her new trainers on without a second thought, she almost fell half-way down the stairs again, grabbing the rail as her toes slipped around unexpectedly in the extra space.

Calm down, Lucy, act normal. There was a different priority here. She took a deep breath and walked steadily the last few steps, peeking round into the living room.

"Back in half an hour, Mum."

"OK, love." Mum hadn't touched the sandwich yet. She was staring at the telly. Which wasn't on.

Lucy looked at her watch. 10:34 a.m. Back by 11:04. It would be important to keep this promise to Mum. She knew that. Thirty minutes. Right. Go.

Lucy sauntered as slowly as she could to the back door, stepping outside and closing the door gently. A soft click. Then she ran, pelting up the path using the tree roots as starting blocks. Out into the meadow and up the hill. It felt so good to run, to move. Her heart beat against her chest and the damp air licked cold on her cheeks, now rosy with exercise. The energy she was keeping trapped inside her released through her skin. She held her arms out, setting it free. There were no lies here. No secrets. The Yew was there, majestic and sturdy, looking into her, knowing her without her needing to speak a word.

But the meadow was just a meadow. Green and damp and beautiful, but nothing magical. Among the fairy circles, there were tiny new mushrooms pushing up beside their parents. New members of a silent community, their hats respectfully bowing to each other. But they were just mushrooms. She paused under the Yew. The broken branch was still broken, but the stump had healed. A scar, but no longer bleeding sap. Lucy put her hand on it, feeling the rough bark scraping her fingers, dusty and sticky.

There was a fizz, like static. Of course, she needed to let them know she was here.

Lucy leaned down and undid the Velcro on her trainers. Pulling off her socks, she placed a foot on the dry dirt by the Yew. The effect was immediate. The electricity shot up her calf and she could feel the roots of her hair lifting. The bark of the tree shifted, and then the old woman was there, rubber boots clomping towards her, yet the blades of grass beneath them did not stir. Her hands were in her pockets, and escaped hair moved against her neck. The branches of the Yew shadowed her face as she approached. The bandages on her arm had gone.

"You got my message, then," said Ceinwen.

15

The Changing

Ceinwen's hair sparkled with dew. She smelled earthy, like the Yew.

"Hi, Ceinwen, I came as soon as I could, but I only have half an hour. Mum said."

"Time is negotiable," she stated. "We have people to see, but they are hard to get to."

"Who?"

"The Council have summoned me. And you. But first we must change into suitable attire." She winked, and the corner of her mouth wrinkled. Lucy looked down at her jeans, wondering if she should have chosen smarter clothes.

Looking back up at Ceinwen, she noticed that the smile on her lips was widening.

Then fur began growing on Ceinwen's cheeks, and the wisps of hair under her rain hood started dancing, locks plaiting together forming tall towers on the top of her head. Her arms lengthened out, touching the ground, and her fingers shortened to nubs. Suddenly, she shrank. Her clothes disappeared, leaving a glossy grey hide, sinewy muscles and strong hind legs.

She was a hare.

"It was you! That day in the meadow! I saw you!"

"Indeed, it was." The hare chuckled and licked her paw delicately. Pink tongue exploring her short fingers.

"But you can still talk?"

"Well, it's only a different outfit. It's still me."

"Oh." Lucy didn't really think this explained what just happened, but felt she didn't really know enough to ask any more questions. She had an urge to write something on her Post-it Notes, and went to pull them from her pocket. No. There was no time for that. Some questions needed to stay unanswered. At least today.

"Right, so what are you going to wear?" Ceinwen looked her up and down, her whiskers twitching. "Where do you feel your power most?"

"Erm. What do you mean?"

"You are sensitive to the magic here, yes?"

"Yes, I suppose so. It's strongest in my feet, but I can feel it through my hands, especially if I close my eyes."

"Hmm. Yes. Vibration through the skin. What do you feel when you put your hands on the earth?"

Lucy bent down and placed her hands palm down onto the ground. Closing her eyes, she tried to concentrate. Instantly, she imagined a beetle scurrying along the grass and an earthworm squirming through the soil. She could feel the grass roots holding on with white fingers spreading through the loam. Deeper down she could feel a thrum. Like millions of signals, passing under her. She gasped. The ground under her was mapped out in her head. Each vibration she sensed gave her an image of the creature or plant. It wasn't imagination at all.

"Wow. I can feel everything."

"Try humming. Keep your eyes closed." Ceinwen watched her, mustard eyes glistening.

Lucy took a breath and hummed. Low and long, her throat rumbled, and she could feel the sound curling around her skull and tickling the top of her nose. Instantly, the area she could sense underground widened. She could see the whole meadow. Everything was lit, and the closer the creature the brighter it was in her mind, like a moving picture behind her eyelids. At the edge of the meadow, a family of rabbits slept in a burrow. A clump of buttercups to her right chatted to each other through their roots. And underpinning it all, the Yew's long dark limbs stretched out under her feet, deep into the earth. All the plants were connected, passing messages underground, tendrils reaching and exploring. Microscopic bacteria squirmed, dying and growing, reaching out and then withdrawing again, connecting one root to another, and then breaking and joining again elsewhere.

Lucy's lungs emptied and she stopped humming. Immediately her brain map shrank to a few feet around her. She lifted her hands up, frightened of the power she had. Opening her eyes, she looked at Ceinwen whose hare eyes, yellow and staring, were locked onto her face.

"So? How far could you go?"

"To the edge of the meadow. Why? How? How can I do that? What is it? I—"

"It seems you are very powerful indeed, Lucy. It won't be long before you can ask the earth to bend to your will. I knew you were different. You're one of us."

Lucy was flabbergasted. All these years she had struggled to fit in. All those places she couldn't go because she was too sensitive. To the lights, the sounds, the smells, the people. All the conversations she couldn't follow, because there was always some unknown script of body language and social rules that no one ever gave her the instructions for, but got angry when she didn't know what to do. It seemed that the very things that made her struggle were the very things that gave her power. Here, she was understood, and she understood the meadow and its creatures. Even the humming had a use! Danny always said there was power in music. Little did he know he was right, literally! Here, in this medium-sized, unassuming meadow. Little Lucy had found out the significance of it. She had found it by simply walking through it. Lucy's heart seemed to swell with pride in her chest. She was home at last.

"OK. Now we know what your power is, let's see which animal suits you best. Stick your fingers in your ears. I'll give you a bit of help to start off with."

"What? Why?"

"Just do what I ask. Trust me." Ceinwen placed her paws on Lucy's feet. She could feel the pads pushing firmly down onto her bare skin. Although Ceinwen was only a couple of feet tall, the full weight of her human form was still there. It really was just an outfit after all, Lucy thought. She stuck her forefingers into her ears. The sounds of the meadow around her muffled.

"Right, so close your eyes and hum. Like before."

Lucy did as she was told. She could feel Ceinwen's claws harder now, pushing her toes into the ground. They felt as if they were splaying out under the pressure, tendons flicking over each other. It was a sort of pain she recognised, the same pain that you had when your shoes were too small, sort of comforting.

Then she felt herself drop to the ground. Her clothes seemed to fall away, but yet she could still feel the weight of the blanket over her shoulders. She gasped as she felt the damp morning air brush her skin.

"Keep humming! We're not finished yet."

Lucy took another breath and concentrated on that low rumble in her throat. The sound that had comforted her for so long. The sound that drowned out the world. Then her breath ran out.

"Right. Open your eyes, then."

Lucy looked. Ceinwen now towered above her and she had to crane her neck to see up to her. At first she thought that she was seeing a giant hare, taller than the cottage, but no, it was she who had shrunk. Her eyesight was blurry, and the daylight seemed far too bright. She looked at her hands. They were no longer hands, and they were huge! Large fleshy palms with short but lethal claws. Her thick arms were covered in black velvet. Her chest and waist heaved as she breathed, all covered in silky fur. She put a paw onto her face. Her nose was pointed and wrinkly and her forehead disappeared back onto her scalp, again covered in the softest fur she had ever felt.

"Am I…a mole?"

"You are indeed." Ceinwen chuckled. "Were you expecting something else?"

Lucy had to admit that she was a little disappointed. Moles didn't seem to be the most glamorous or useful animal. They were mostly blind and couldn't run very fast. What use could she be?

"Well, I suppose if you're needing a hole dug, I'm your girl."

Ceinwen laughed loud. It echoed off the bark of the Yew and vibrated against Lucy's velvet skin.

"I think you'll be surprised what you can do, my friend." She loped off towards the other side of the Yew, bouncing over a tree root, hind legs flipping up, briefly revealing the pure white underfur on her tail. "Well, are you coming or not?"

Lucy looked at her paws again and noted that she had an extra thumb on each hand. She wiggled it and it tingled.

For Danny, she thought, and waddled as quickly as she could after Ceinwen.

16

The Gathering

Puck stood, leaning against his chair, a gnarled thing made of oak. He cleared his throat.

"Welcome." He spoke quietly, but with a gravitas that seemed to make everyone hear.

The room, which was initially filled with the sound of low conversation, gradually waned to a few voices, then rustling quiet. Puck waited patiently.

"I know you are all concerned about how this came about, but we must think forward, and of our plan to solve the problem, not spend time laying blame on a human who did not know any better."

The room mumbled agreement. Some forty individuals were sitting at carved tables and chairs made of roots that could be a thousand years old, from trees long since disappeared from the ground above. There was a raised platform at one end made of packed earth. Lit by a blueish glow from several lamps in the ceiling, the room was dusty with age and tradition, formally arranged, and yet naturally sculpted from roots and packed soil. It was warm, heated by the bodies that occupied it, but also by its proximity to the earth's centre, deep underground. It was a natural cave made larger by use.

A figure rose from his seat at the front, cloaked in a brown hooded garment that reached to the floor, and used a broad stick to steady himself. The skin on his hand was grey and scaled. The room looked on respectfully as he started to speak.

"You must understand, my friend, that we do not discuss the recent events to lay blame, but to discover how they came about. With this knowledge we can establish the best course of action. We must be fully aware of the powers at work here. There are humans involved, and that means our very secrecy and lives are at stake."

"I respectfully agree, your grace, but there is a time for discussion, and a time for action. We have delayed more than we should already. Gwyllgi has taken an innocent—"

"Not an innocent. He damaged a Sentinel!" There were raised voices in agreement. Nodding heads. Wagging fingers from those who disagreed.

"Without knowledge of the consequences. He is still an innocent and should be treated as such."

Murmurs echoed from the walls again. Then a click of a door from the back made all bodies turn. Chairs scraped and cloaks stirred against skin.

Ceinwen strode forward, changing to her human form as she did so, growing taller with each step, confident with her right to be there. A small mole followed, startled with the sudden mass of people before her.

"We have a sensitive among us. Please respect her needs." Ceinwen's voice rang out.

As the echo of her call rang out, the room parted, silently allowing a wide walkway. The tables and chairs no longer scraped, but slid as if on rails. Every figure looked away and towards the stage, eyes down.

Lucy looked behind her to see whether there was some kind of royal person entering the room, but no one was there.

"It's OK, Lucy, this is for you, to make you comfortable. There is nothing to fear." Ceinwen touched her shoulder with slightly more pressure than usual, and Lucy's skin began to tingle and heat up. She grew, and felt her clothes returning as if she were stepping out of a cold pool into warm air. She looked at her hands. Fur was retreating away up her arms and disappearing under the folds of the blanket. The extra thumb had shrunk away into the side of her palm. She was Lucy again. But then, she always had been, just in a different form.

She looked to the room in front of her. There were no eyes on her, there was ample space for her to move, and there was no noise. This was OK. She stepped forward. Nothing happened, so she took another few steps. Ceinwen smiled and strode to the raised platform, climbing some steps hewn into the dense soil. Lucy followed, not believing that she could enter a room where all attention was on her, yet not on her. And more so, that these people knew enough about her that they knew how to help. Knew what to do to make this OK. For her.

She climbed the steps and stood next to Ceinwen.

"Are you ready?" she said.

"I think so. Erm, ready for what?"

Ceinwen nodded, and the room allowed themselves to look up.

Immediately, Lucy felt the rush of attention, of the eyes on her, brushing her skin as if with tiny fingers, reaching even from the back of the room. She took a breath, and without really knowing what she was doing, started humming quietly. The 'eye fingers' immediately withdrew and formed an invisible net in front of her, as if cowed, hesitating a few inches away. It was OK, Lucy could control this. She could protect herself. She was using a power she never knew she had.

"Hello, Lucy. Thank you so much for coming." Puck smiled from his corner chair, encouraging her to keep her eyes on him, something to concentrate on. Heads around the room nodded in agreement, but silently, as if they knew she needed calm. Lucy managed a small smile back.

Ceinwen stepped forward then and raised both hands. "Greetings, friends. You have summoned Lucy to your

Council, understandably given recent occurrences. The Circles have been broken and my protection has been breached. Action is needed, and we are fortunate to have Lucy, even with her powers in their infancy, on our side."

A figure stood in the middle of the room. "But wasn't it her brother who started this?"

Lucy looked at Ceinwen in alarm. "What does he mean? This wasn't Danny's fault, he was just angry. He didn't mean to break that branch... He had no idea what it meant!"

Ceinwen placed a rough hand on her arm and smiled softly.

"Thank you, friend." She turned to the speaker and bowed her head graciously, then looked up. "May I remind you that for centuries, our kind has been hidden. The meadow next to which I have lived all these years is just a meadow to them. The Yew is just a tree. The Fairy Circles are just mushrooms with a lovely old story. Many believe that the circles signify the roof of fairy ballrooms, and that we dance to eternal music underground!"

There was a wave of low laughter stretching to the back of the room.

"They have no idea of the connections under the earth and how far they reach. Only recently have humans used their science to find out what we have known since the beginning of time. Of the connections between all beings, plants, insects, and creatures, they know nothing."

Lucy stepped forward, shaking. They didn't know her brother. They didn't know how kind and patient he was. One moment of anger had made them judge him like a criminal. And yes, to him, it was just a tree. A majestic one, but still just a tree. Just a branch, something to take out his anger so that he wouldn't do something he regretted. Rather a branch than his sister.

"Wait." Lucy's voice sounded thin in the large room. "Danny would not have known. No one would have known." She turned again to Puck. "I didn't know! These things I can do, the powers. I didn't know I had them. We just moved to the cottage at the edge of meadow. We moved here for me. We didn't know." Lucy clenched her fists and looked straight out into the room. "That…creature has taken my brother. You need to help me get him back." Her eyes stung and the room started to blur.

Puck turned to those gathered.

"We need to act now."

17

The Attack

Ceinwen's tail bobbed in front of her in the tunnel, the same way they had come, the same grey soil. Lucy could sense the insects, worms, burrowing things on the other side of the wall, squirming and wriggling, searching for food, shelter, company. The damp seeped and felt cold against her fur. She closed her eyes and hummed again, picking up the area around them. They were still deep. Her throat's vibration stopped and her senses returned to tunnel walls.

"I think you made an impression." Ceinwen's voice strained from ahead, dirt muffled. She turned briefly towards her. Lucy stayed quiet. She was thinking of Danny.

"You did well." But even through her hare face, Lucy could see Ceinwen was disappointed with the Council's reaction.

Ceinwen turned a corner and the floor started to slope upwards. Lucy followed, mole paws scrabbling to keep up. She had more room because of her size, but still didn't have a hare's speed.

They had travelled for what felt like about two hours, through this tunnel and that, detouring past roots and the dank homes of ground-loving creatures, Lucy recognising the same return route back to the meadow. Ceinwen had assured her that she would be back within the time limit her mother had told her, but at this point it seemed impossible.

Then Lucy felt a movement, like an earthquake. A sudden pressure above. Her throat rumbled automatically, searching for the source of the feeling. Ceinwen didn't stop; she hadn't felt it.

In her mind picture, a set of teeth followed by clammy grey skin was clawing down at them.

"Ceinwen, wait, there's something…"

The hare stopped, turned awkwardly back. "What? What do you hear?"

"Something. With teeth. It's grey and it wants us. It's coming from over there. I…I saw it in my head." Lucy used her paw to point upwards to the right. The tunnel had headed under a dip here and the earth surface was only a few feet from them. Dust fell from the tunnel roof, and Ceinwen ducked instinctively. Claws out, she waited. Then in seconds the passage collapsed. Soil, stones and roots rained down on them both, followed by snapping jaws dripping with saliva.

"BACK!" Ceinwen shouted, and Lucy crawled backwards as swiftly as she could with the little space available, no time to turn. She put her wide paws over her head and instinctively made herself as small as possible.

Ceinwen's teeth were bared, and she leaped forward and onto the neck of the creature, whose body was now halfway into the tunnel, sinewy hind legs clawing at the earth to get to them. Her fangs dug deep into the flesh and fur, drips of blood leaked, soaked up by the dirty, matted fur around the wound. The creature writhed, snapping its jaws at Ceinwen. She yelped and leaped back as a free claw scraped her shoulder, breaking the skin.

Then Lucy screamed. It came from her stomach, using all the air in her lungs. Pure terror radiated out from her in a sound she had never heard herself make. Ceinwen retreated further, dark blood dripping from her lips, as the grey being was sucked back up through the hole it had torn through. The soil was moving in slivers. Beetles appeared though the surface, millipedes and earwigs, worms and woodlice, all scurrying frantically, rushing at the attacker like a miniature army. The creature was covered, pushed back, its limbs trying to scrape the insects away from its jaws. The hole was shrinking, the battle was drawing away from them, up and out. Soon the tunnel roof had returned, and the only evidence of the attack was the panting chest of Ceinwen, and the bloody saliva caught in the fur of her paws. Lucy's scream petered out, and with the last of the sound she closed her eyes, checking her mind picture. Whatever it was had been sent to the daylight above and was scrabbling unsuccessfully at the ground over them, frustration in its yellow eyes. It howled.

Ceinwen looked at her in awe as Lucy thumbed the dust from her lips.

18

The Gwyllgi

"That damn hare." The dog paced, fur moving slowly against him, as if through water, black as coal and matted with old blood.

Danny sat by him in the shade of a knotted hedge, eyes misted and unseeing, his head on his folded knees. He stared at his shoes, caked in mud and sodden. He felt cold. So cold. The clothes he wore stuck to his skin and he felt every breath of chill through them. His hands felt numb, his fingertips raw and the back of his neck throbbed as though some great hand was placed there, weighing him down and controlling every pulse of his blood.

He had no idea how he'd got there. One minute he was running in the meadow, trying to clear his head. Trying to get out of breath and squeeze the anger from his chest. Then his hands were on a branch. He was straining at his muscles to release it. To break something, anything, to stop the rage. Then a flash, and two eyes, drawing him in. He was helpless. A rag doll with no control over his own limbs. Drawn towards a creature such as he had never seen before, by an invisible cord that had knotted around his chest. Then this. Just darkness, and cold. So much cold.

The creature turned to him and smiled, a green mist oozing through the gaps in his teeth.

"She may have thwarted this small attempt, but she had no chance at stopping me freeing myself from the circles. Not with your help, human." He laughed, loud and long and his voice echoed and bounced around Danny's brain. He licked at the sap between his claws, recently stolen from a downed pine, felled with one sweep just an hour ago.

"Over one hundred years I've been imprisoned by those damn mushrooms. She took a hundred years of my life. I'll be taking hers in return, believe you me."

Gwyllgi turned again and paced another line in the dirt. The grass rotted under his step, veins of filth radiated from his footprints and daubed the ground. The earth had blackened around them and the hedge had started to wilt.

"That Puck." He spat the name as if poisoned by the very sound of it. "And the Council. They will not know chaos like I will wield upon this world. What say you, human?!"

Danny looked up at him, head lolling, drunk with the darkness that filled him. A forced rasp left his parched lips: "Yes. I will do what you say."

"Of course you will, human. Your will is so weak. Your race disgusts me. How is it that you control this world with your weak thoughts and your simple machines?" The dog scoffed. Snarling and dripping, he continued to pace, hate emanating from every hair on his thick hide. "Out of all my followers, you are the most useful."

Danny's head flopped again onto his knees. Inside he was desperate, trapped within himself. It was as if he were continually falling down a deep mine, nothing to grab on to and no control. His head ached and his throat was raw. It was all he could do to hold just one thought: Lucy. Lucy. Lucy. Lucy. Repeating inside his brain. If he could just hold on to that word, there was hope.

19

The Return

Ceinwen's snout finally reached the crisp morning air by the Yew. Scrambling out, she shook the soil from her fur, wincing at the open scratch on her shoulder.

"Come on up then, Lucy. You're safe here."

Lucy's mole paws appeared from the hole. The air smelled the same as it had when they had first dived into the earth what seemed like hours ago.

"What time is it?" Lucy asked, hoping dearly that she would be able to think of a good excuse for her mother, who would doubtless be frantic with worry.

Ceinwen stretched her lean limbs skyward. "I did say that time was…negotiable, didn't I? Don't worry, you will make it back within the allotted minutes." Her stretch continued further than it should as her body lengthened, fur disappearing to reveal the familiar old coat and wellies. Lucy closed her eyes, stretched her paws out as far as she could reach and thought, "Lucy". Opening her eyes, she saw the ground rushing away from her and there appeared her feet, bare toes in the dirt, scrunching up with the chill. She reached for her shoes and socks, safe, if a little damp, by the Yew's trunk.

"You're getting good at that quickly," Ceinwen commented as she drew her hood up around her face. She had a slightly strange look in her eye. Almost frightened, as though she saw Lucy differently now. "Did you notice that the creature in the tunnel did not see you? I think the blanket helped." She put her hand inside her coat, feeling for the new wound to protect it from rubbing against her clothes.

"What happens now?" The Council had been attentive to them, but stalwart in their refusal to act. Just as in the human world, there seemed to be endless questions and procedures to wade through.

"They're worried, but they haven't experienced Gwyllgi as Puck and I have. They do not understand him. They do not understand what he is capable of." She let out a long sigh and shook her head. "I think we're on our own."

Lucy despaired. She had seen them battle that creature. She had seen them fail, and she had seen it take her brother. What could she add to this? What could they possibly do without help? It was hopeless.

"Tonight, as the sun sets, we shall start to travel. To find your brother."

"What about Mum?" Lucy knew there was no way she'd be letting Lucy out after dark. Not today, not with her brother missing. She was starting to think it was pointless, them even trying to save Danny.

"It's not something I like to do, but I do have a way of making your mother unaware you have gone. It only lasts a short time, but it should be enough."

"Tonight, then. Here?" Lucy scuffed the toe of her trainer against the ground.

"Yes." Ceinwen paused and breathed out heavily through her nose, turned away and then paused. "What you did, in the tunnel," She shifted her weight and her Wellington boots squeaked against each other. "Have you ever done anything like that before?"

Lucy thought hard. She had screamed before, but it had always been an inward sort of noise. It was a strange thought, but she had always been trying to escape, trying to run. She'd heard of others like her hitting out, pure anxiety directed at anyone who was close by, but Lucy, she always went into herself, trying to shut out the world. It was the first time she'd directed her feelings towards someone—or something—else. She had never wanted to hurt anyone. Never wanted to lash out. So she'd always locked it deep inside and just run.

"Er, no. I've had the feeling before, but I've just always squashed it down into my tummy." It sounded ridiculous when she said it like that, but that was how it felt.

The wind caught Ceinwen's hair and made it dance around her hood. It looked like miniature ladies in long hair-dresses circling around her face, waving their medieval wing-sleeves. Ceinwen was magical. It seeped from her, as if she couldn't help but let it out. This was why she was calm. She could just be herself. No need to trap her emotions inside. The meadow and its creatures accepted her as she was. This place needed her just as she was. Even though she was trapped in this place as a protector and guardian, always being called to return, Lucy felt she was the freest person she'd ever met.

"As I thought." And with that, she was gone, striding out towards her cottage, fists planted firmly in pockets.

Lucy watched her open the gate, then turned and ran down the hill.

20

The Visitor

Mum was still on the sofa when Lucy arrived back. Glancing at the clock on the microwave as she entered the kitchen door, she saw it was exactly 11.04 a.m. Ceinwen was right, time could stretch sometimes.

"I'm back, Mum."

"Oh, hi, Luce. Nice walk?"

"Yes, thanks, Mum. It's a nice day." Lucy regretted saying that. It sounded overly cheery, like she'd forgotten about Danny. Keeping all the events of the last fourteen hours from Mum was hard. Lucy wasn't one to reveal everything going on in her head, but there was an urge to tell all, to share her thoughts. To share the load. But Lucy knew that the first questions Mum would ask would be,

'Who are these people? Are they safe? Where's Danny? How do they know where Danny is?'

To be honest, in Mum's position, she'd be asking the same. She imagined herself saying, 'So there's this big evil dog thing that was trapped by a ring of mushrooms, but he's escaped and captured Danny, and this tiny human and an old lady in wellies are going to help me find him. Oh, and by the way, I can turn into a mole.' It would never work. She would never believe her, and if she thought Lucy was going mad, she'd never let her leave the house.

Moreover, the questions would be just too much. Sometimes giving information was a lot easier than taking it in, but if you talked, people always talked back, and Lucy's brain wasn't designed to soak it all in. Not all at once.

"Hmm." Mum went back to staring at the blank telly screen again. The ham sandwich was still there. Lucy relaxed a little. Mum hadn't even noticed what she'd said. Or how she'd said it.

"Do you want that sandwich?" Lucy eyed it. She'd forgotten to eat breakfast at all, and her stomach was starting to make those horrible squeaky noises. It may have only been thirty minutes for Mum, but Lucy had been away for hours.

"Go ahead, love. Thanks for making it, but I'm just too worried to eat." Her eyes returned to the blank screen.

Lucy picked up the plate and sat next to her on the sofa, taking a large bite and chewing slowly. Food felt good. She had a notion that she'd drained some of her energy that morning. It made sense. All that power had to come from somewhere. The ham sandwich disappeared quickly, and Lucy headed to the kitchen for an apple. Then there was a knock on the front door. After a moment of confusion in her face, Mum gasped.

"Oh God, it's Mum. Danny must not have ordered her a taxi!"

Mum leaped up from the sofa to get the door.

"So sorry, Mum, I totally forgot, let me get that bag." Grandma stood in the doorway looking as though she was about to explode, but then her face changed.

"What are you doing here? I thought it was just Danny and Lucy?" Mum couldn't hold it in any longer and let out a huge sob.

"Oh my goodness, what's happened? Let me in, come on, give me a hug. Gracious me, you're so upset! Where's Lucy? Where's Danny?"

Lucy stood in the hall. "Hello, Grandma," she said, changing weight from left foot to right foot, and awkwardly looking at Grandma's cardigan buttons.

"Danny's gone, Mum. He left Lucy on her own last night and he's disappeared. I've had the police round, but they were useless. Mum, I'm so worried."

"OK, love, come and sit down. Tell me everything."

Lucy felt the knot in her stomach again. The ham sandwich was swirling, and she looked at the apple in her hand thinking it might not be a good idea. She hated seeing people upset, but especially Mum. Everyone thought that Lucy couldn't feel it. That she ran away from it because she didn't know what it was. Actually, it was the opposite. Lucy could feel every bit. Ten times worse. It was like seeing one person cry meant that her whole body was crying. The pores on her skin felt clammy and her lungs went tight. She just needed to get away from it before she imploded into herself. She remembered her scream. That's what happened when she let it out. Until she could control it, she would need to keep it inside. At least this was something she was well practiced at.

She ran upstairs. Grandma was here, she'd help Mum. Lucy needed to save her energy for something bigger. She needed to save Danny. She needed to eat this apple. She needed to rest.

Heading to her room, laying the blanket carefully over the end of her bed, she kicked off her trainers and sat cross legged at the pillow end. She took a deep breath, needing to process. Needing to let her thoughts settle. She picked up a book, one of her favourites that she must have read twenty times. Opening it at random, she let herself sink into familiar words. They flowed over her like warm water, gathering together all the chaos in her head and washing away her worry. All the while her big toe gently brushed the edge of the blanket, which had become an old friend.

After a while, and after the apple and a silent hour with the book, Lucy smelled food. Grandma's spaghetti bolognese. She would recognise it anywhere. Mum wasn't crying any more, and she could hear Grandma clattering pans in the kitchen and complaining about the state of the cheese grater. The knot in Lucy's stomach had gone, and she was starting to feel hungry again. Giving the blanket a last pat, she placed her book on it. As she did, the back of her hand brushed against something. Something hard.

Picking up a corner of the blanket, she felt along its edge. Yes, there it was, a small, solid lump. A little way along there was another one, and then another. She spread the blanket out on her bed, gently touching the rough wool all the way around. In all, she counted twenty-seven lumps, all around the same size and all placed an equal distance apart around the edge of the blanket. Bringing one of the lumps up closer to her face, she saw that the wool was woven in two layers. This meant there could be two different patterns on each side of the blanket. Something had been pushed in between the layers.

Gently prying the fibres apart, she managed to push her fingernail into the lump. It felt wooden, and rough. Pushing the strands further apart, she managed to push the object out. It was a cherry stone, slightly oval with a ridge all the way around it. It was a light beige and was obviously quite old as it had started to wrinkle a little. Lucy placed it in her palm and looked at it. Why would someone hide cherry stones in a blanket? There was the cherry tree in the garden; were they from that tree? Someone had spent time washing and gently pushing twenty-seven stones between the strands, but why?

Then Lucy remembered what Puck had said last night. The Cherry was a Sentinel tree, like the Yew. Were these stones from the Sentinel? Was that why they were in the blanket? Who lived in this house all those years ago, and why did they think to put the stones in the blanket?

Just then, Grandma called from the kitchen. "Dinner's on the table, Lucy. Wash your hands, love."

"OK, down in a minute." Lucy shoved the cherry stone in her pocket. She wanted to go to the Cherry, lay her hands on the trunk and see what she could feel with her new powers. After dinner, she would say she needed fresh air. She would go and find out.

21

The Sentinel

Lucy gobbled her spaghetti and asked for seconds. Mum looked at her. "Hungry then, Luce?"

"Erm, yes. Sorry."

Grandma laughed. "Well, she's always liked my spaghetti! You eat as much as you want, dear. Go on, help yourself."

Lucy felt wrong eating. Like she was betraying Danny or something. Mum pushed her food around her plate with worry. Lucy almost felt like she should be doing the same, to show Mum that she was anxious, but she really was ravenous.

Lucy was worried, but it was about different things. Mum was probably thinking about all the horrible things that could have happened to Danny. The worst thing was that Lucy knew exactly what had happened, and it was something that Mum could never have thought of in a million years.

She mixed the sauce in with the spaghetti so that it coated the strands and thought about the weave in the blanket. Suddenly the pasta tasted slightly woolly, as though her thoughts were merging. She had to get out and see that cherry tree.

"I found some tinned peaches in the cupboard. Do you want some?" Grandma collected the plates and put them in the sink.

"No thanks, Grandma, I'm full now."

"She's always been more of a 'savoury' person, haven't you, Luce?" Mum smiled thinly at her, but it still didn't reach her eyes.

"Apart from M&Ms." Lucy pushed her chair back with the back of her legs and stood up.

"Apart from M&Ms." Mum looked away and smiled better this time. "Love you, Luce. You know that, don't you?"

"Yes, Mum. You too." Lucy moved from the table. "Just going in the garden for a bit. That OK?"

"Of course, darling."

Lucy could feel them both watching her as she left. She ran upstairs and found her trainers. They were still a little damp, but she shoved them on anyway without loosening the laces. It was funny how she'd got used to the new ones. She'd put them on without even thinking about them, because, well, she had bigger thoughts, bigger worries. She felt automatically for the packet of Post-it Notes in her pocket, and then paused. This was something that was her comfort, too. Something she could write down her thoughts on. A way of getting them out of her head silently. A way she could say things her way, without comment from others that she was being weird or strange. She made a decision then and placed the Post-it Notes on her bedside table. This was a place to be herself. She would be like Ceinwen. She didn't need to hide any more.

She paused by the blanket, too, placing her hands on the weave. The voices were still there, distant, but in time, not in travel. In fact, it felt as though the voices were coming from the next room. Children playing, someone singing an old song in the kitchen. It wasn't Grandma. She couldn't sing and always joked that she was tone deaf. It was someone long gone, but whose memory was very strong. She mouthed the words of the song. Somehow she knew it. Like she was born knowing it.

Heading out of the front door, her feet crunched on the stones along the path. There were bare patches where the gravel hadn't been topped up. Brown earth, hardened by years of footfall, with a slight sticky layer from the overnight spring rain. As Lucy neared the Cherry, she felt the same as she had in the meadow. The same longing to be nearer the Yew, and the connection with the roots reaching deep underground. She'd not noticed it before, but then she hadn't looked for it before. Her fingertips started buzzing slightly, and the cherry stone, despite being only the size of a large peanut M&M, dug into her thigh from her jeans pocket.

The Cherry Tree was much smaller than the Yew, its long limbs zigzagging out. The blossom had rust-coloured patches, and the scent was sharp and heavy. Should it even be blooming at the moment? She couldn't remember when cherry trees were supposed to come out. She supposed it was probably more likely to be right than the apples she'd seen the day before, however. The bark was grey and wrinkled, and the shape was messy, but at the same time just as it should be, like a bonsai tree; perfectly sculpted into what a tree should look like. The trunk leaned out onto the driveway. Mum had caught it a couple of times with her car bumper and Lucy cringed at the thought that this beautiful being in front of her could not even complain about the bruises it had received.

As Lucy approached, she whispered, ducking the lower branches to get to the centre. "Hello, there, I'm Lucy. I know what you are." Then she closed her eyes as she laid her palm on the bark. She felt the tree shift under her touch, and her mind picture showed the whole thing glowing with bright veins, flowing with movement and life. The veins did not stop at the roots, and Lucy realised that they carried on, under the house and out into the neighbouring field, where sheep grazed, nibbling at the grass tips. It wasn't the roots themselves, but a continuous flow of messages, carried by other roots, other creatures, microscopic living things in the soil. She gasped at the magic of it, but realised that this wasn't just the Sentinel. This was all trees, everywhere. There was a sudden sadness that so many trees had been cut. Been used for furniture and books and scaffolding. No longer able to live with the connections they had with the world.

The main bough that she had ducked to get closer to the middle crept towards her. The tip nuzzled her pocket where the stone was and she suddenly felt a deep love, as though a mother had just found a lost child after many years.

"You know about the blanket, don't you?" The veins tinkled inside her head like tiny bells. "Do you want your stones back?"

The bough withdrew slowly and purposefully, moving up to her chest and touching where her heart was. Lucy instinctively knew what that meant. They were a gift.

"Luce, I'm putting the kettle on. Do you want a cuppa?" Grandma's shrill call through the open window cut through Lucy's thoughts and her eyes snapped open. The tree became still. Lucy felt as though she had been ripped away from sleep.

"Erm, no thanks, Grandma, I'm fine." She felt angry for the disturbance, but knew that Grandma just hadn't realised. It happened all the time. Lucy being lost deep in her thoughts, only to be wrenched away by a mundane question, or a noise that seemed like a rope tightening around her throat. A baby's cry was the worst. It was a sound that made her feel like her head was in a food mixer.

Lucy sighed, looking up to the sky through the stirring branches, heavy perfume wafting and mixing with the aroma of wet grass. The tree had left her. She had lost the connection. She felt for the stone in her pocket, and as she hooked her fingers around it, she felt like a protector. These stones were a gift to her, and were what gave the blanket its true power. She decided then that she would guard it for the rest of her life.

22

The Black Dog

Danny shrank back as the green mist seeped through the air towards him.

"No, please no!" He held his hands up in front of his face, as if not seeing the creature's jaws approaching would stop them.

One word repeated on his lips: Lucy, Lucy, Lucy. He whispered it, as quietly as he could manage, but loud enough to reassure himself that he still could. As though the word itself was the only thing keeping him from going mad.

The creature paused, breath stinking of rot and death. "Who is Lucy?"

Danny froze. God, no, he couldn't tell. Would he go after her? He mustn't let that happen. Little Lucy. His little sis. It was his job to protect her and he'd failed. He must at least find the strength for this. His lips fell silent and with the tiny drop of energy he had left, he glared. Defiant. Clamping his mouth shut and looking straight into the eyes of the creature.

It roared.

Threads of spittle flung from his jowls and were carried by a gust of foul air. He stamped his front paw to the ground and leaped towards him as if to attack, teeth stopping just millimetres from Danny's face.

"You. Are. MINE!" he screamed. Eyes blazing, he let the mist from his throat entangle his black tongue and bleed out. Its tendrils filled Danny's nostrils and burned his throat. His whole body spasmed as he fought against it, but it was no use. The great Black Dog had him under his power. His mind was no longer his own. He was a mere puppet for this monster to do with what he wished. With that, Danny blacked out.

Gwyllgi's head snapped round as he heard a sound behind him, the slow rustle of clawed feet crushing dead grass, and the creak of sinew against bone.

"It's about time you showed up." A deep rumble exuded from his neck as he glared at the approaching beasts.

Three grey mastiffs appeared, furless, their grey skin showing seeping sores.

"Massssster," they hissed in unison, their voices as one, their eyes clouded. Their movements were slow and ghostlike as they padded ever closer, muscles writhing under their reptilian hides.

"I did not release you to fail me as you did today. Prove you are loyal and do as I wish."

The mastiffs bowed their heads. "We are sssorry, Masssssssster."

Gwyllgi turned back to Danny, placing a rank paw on his chest, claw tips piercing his thin t-shirt, but he didn't feel them. In an instant they were gone, leaving the corner of the field blackened, silent and devoid of all life.

23

The Dusk

It was getting chilly now, and Lucy shivered in her t-shirt sleeves. She looked up into the branches once more and then turned back to the house.

She was immediately greeted by an eerie face hanging in the air an inch from her nose.

"Ah!" Lucy jumped and scraped her head on the rough bark. She silently apologised to the Sentinel for bumping into it.

"Meet me at the meadow gate at eight o'clock." Ceinwen's voice floated at her, and then the mist face dissipated as she had seen it do before, leaving the nose remaining. She poked at it with her finger, and it too melted into nothing. Rubbing her scalp where a sore lump was forming, Lucy headed back along the path. So, at eight o'clock things would start happening. The nerves started to churn in her stomach.

As she entered the house, Grandma met her at the doorway to the kitchen. "Are you sure you're OK, love?"

"I'm fine, Grandma." Grandma's forehead furrowed into lines. "I'm worried about Danny, though," Lucy added, swiftly. "Is Mum all right?"

Grandma nodded and shuffled back to the kitchen to start loading the dishes into the dishwasher. Lucy mentally kicked herself. She'd obviously sounded too happy or something. She always got that wrong, and people had that same confused look. Lucy recognised it all too well.

There seemed to be a million ways to say the same thing according to how you stood, or how your face was, or whether you said one word higher and another lower. To be honest, she didn't really know why she'd said 'fine'; it seemed to be the 'normal' answer to 'How are you?', like some predefined script, whether you felt fine or not. Once, she'd tried to answer with, 'Actually, I'm a little tingly, and I can feel the label in my jumper', but apparently telling the truth made her weird.

There was nothing she could do about it now. Padding up the stairs and into her room, Lucy tried to think what she would need to take with her. She wasn't sure whether they would be travelling as people, or in their animal shapes. She wondered if Puck had an animal shape. More to the point, Lucy wasn't sure if it was possible to carry anything while she was a mole anyway. Her clothes and the blanket had stayed with her, almost as a layer under her fur. Like Ceinwen had said, it was just a different outfit, worn over her like a cloak. Now that she knew what the blanket meant, and what the stones were, that would be her most important item. But what else? She had no idea how long it would take to rescue Danny, or how they would achieve it. Would she need food? Pyjamas? No, that would be ridiculous. Toothbrush?!

In the end, Lucy decided that there was nothing she owned that could be of use. As she sat on her bed, she saw the packet of Post-it Notes on her bedside table. The question she had written just hours before was still there, in her neat handwriting. She carefully peeled the top note from the pack and stuck it to her bed post. Then after a pause, put the notes and pen into her pocket. She wasn't ready to leave them behind just yet. Lucy picked up her book again and waited.

After looking at her clock for the twenty-third time, it finally showed 7:52 p.m., the time Lucy had planned to go downstairs and ask if she could walk up to the meadow. She had heard Mum call the police officer again, and then a frustrated rant accompanied by Grandma's soothing tones. She realised then how frustrating it was to not be able to do anything, to feel powerless, and to be relying on other people for help. She thought back to the phone call she had overheard and wondered how on earth Mum had coped with it all these years. All the calls she'd made and the emails she'd written. All for her. Months and months of waiting. At least Lucy could do something. To try and save Danny.

Taking a deep breath, she pulled on her trainers and her thickest hoodie, and draped the blanket over her shoulders. Having worn it around the house, clutching a book, for a couple of weeks, she hoped Mum wouldn't think it too unusual for her to be heading out into the garden with it.

"Are you cold, Luce?" Grandma said as Lucy entered the living room.

"Erm, no, I just like the blanket. It's nice and heavy," she said.

"Oh." Grandma shrugged. "Well, if that's what you like, then that's what you like, I suppose."

Mum was sitting on the very edge of the sofa with the house phone in one hand and her mobile in the other. She was rocking gently on her toes, shoulders hunched. There was a full cup of tea on the coffee table, but there was no steam curling from it. Lucy had not seen Mum rock like that before. It was almost as if…

"I just can't wait any more, Mum," she said, and her eyes started getting wet again. Lucy went over to her and placed a hand on the back of her shoulder. Her skin fizzed and Mum flinched slightly.

"He'll come back, Mum, don't worry." Mum looked up at her and managed a thin smile. Then looked down at her mobile, making sure the volume was up for what must have been the thousandth time. Grandma rubbed Mum's back, her palm rustling the fabric of Mum's blouse. Lucy shivered, the rough sound setting her on edge.

"I'm just popping up to the meadow gate to get some fresh air. I won't be long." The lie hung in the air in front of her, and her stomach swirled.

"OK, love. Just ten minutes. Don't go past the gate, will you? I want you to be able to hear if we call."

"I won't, Grandma."

Lucy clicked the back door behind her and turned towards the path. The breeze was damp with a slight smell of wood smoke, and the sun was like a tangerine balancing on the branches of the trees. Bruise-coloured clouds drifted against a pink sky, and the birds had stopped singing.

24

The Bewitching

As Lucy approached the gate, it opened for her, and a gentle breeze seemed to push her up onto the billowing grass. Ceinwen was leaning against a fence post the same colour as her coat. She was so still that you would not have known she was there if you hadn't been looking for her. Hands in her pockets, she fitted into this landscape as though she was part of it. Like she'd grown up from the ground, from hidden roots, to join the surrounding bushes in bathing in the sunset.

"How's ya mother coping?" Ceinwen's gruff voice floated from her hood.

"Not great." Lucy drew the blanket around her and approached the fence to join her. "Grandma's there now."

"Hmm. It'll be harder to put two into a dream-sleep. We'll have less time."

Lucy hadn't thought of that.

"Sorry, I should have warned you." Although she wasn't sure how she could possibly have contacted Ceinwen over the last few hours without looking suspicious. Ceinwen paused, and then took her hands out of her pockets.

"Where were they when you left?"

"In the living room, on the sofa. I think they'll still be there, unless Grandma is making a cup of tea or—"

"Fine," Ceinwen stated. "Stand aside."

She raised her arms out in front of her and closed her eyes. Between her palms appeared a ball of mist, about the size of an apple. It swirled gently around as though trapped inside an invisible globe. Ceinwen was muttering something in a whisper. It sounded like a poem or some sort of spoken lullaby. The words were rhythmic, and the mist started to pulse in time, getting thicker and thicker. Suddenly, as if her ears had been blocked and now they were open, Lucy could understand.

I call on Ceridwen, and the marsh mists
Labour for me, long as you like.
Weave me a dream, sweet Ceridwen
For we have work to do.

Come to me, Ceridwen, she of the valley
Bind me a tale on the wind.
Ceridwen, blind the eyes and silence the tongue
For we have work to do.

Ceinwen blew gently onto the mist and it floated serenely towards the cottage, glowing softly against the dark green of the trees. Lucy watched as it disappeared around the bend of the path.

"It won't hurt them, will it?"

"No, of course not." Ceinwen rubbed her palms on her coat and headed up the hill towards the Yew. "They'll lose a few hours, but they'll wake feeling rested."

Lucy trotted after her, working hard to keep up. "Who's Ceridwen?"

Ceinwen stopped suddenly and stared into Lucy's eyes. They burned into her and she had to look away.

"Your power is strong, girl. To understand th' old language with no teachin'." She turned and started walking up the slope again. "Ceridwen is…was…an ancestor o' mine. She could use the water in the air and in the ground, make it do 'er will." The corners of her mouth creased into a tiny smile. "Like me," she added. "There's a certain advantage to humans being made up of mostly water, too. A little extra moisture in their ears 'n eyes can do wonders. Not that I make a habit of bewitching humans, y'understand."

Lucy nodded. She felt an enormous guilt sitting in her gut, but what else could they do? This way, at least, her family would be safe while they found Danny.

25

The Night

"Delicious!" The Black Dog curled his lips, thick tongue wetting the already bloody fur. He arched his back, stretching out, and then sprawling. His claws dug into the soil, and inky stains spread from him and out into a nearby hedge, which shrank back into a twisted mat of dead twigs and rotting leaves. The stench carried to Danny, who gagged on it, but nothing came out. He'd not been allowed to eat or drink for a day. His stomach was empty.

"What's the matter, human? Was that not an enjoyable experience for you?"

Danny sank to his knees and ran his fingers through his hair. His head ached, and he couldn't see. The world was just a blur and he felt like his limbs weren't his own. The monster's voice floated into his consciousness. The very sound of it made him nauseated. His body felt half there, half still falling into that never-ending pit. Looking up, he managed to whisper, "Please, please let me go."

Gwyllgi's laugh echoed and his fur floated around him with a life of its own.

"I'm not done with you yet, boy." He licked the grease from his paws. "You are too useful a puppet."

He poked a single claw to the ground, skewering a beetle. The insect flailed its legs as it entered the beast's mouth. He crunched through its shell and then searched the ground for another.

An hour before, they had been standing at the front door of a house in a nearby town, while a family cowered in their living room. A crowd of people had chanted, with fists balled, at the house. Horrible names, ancient slurs, bigoted shouts of hate, at a family who had done nothing wrong. Danny had led them there, with Gwyllgi putting the words into his mouth. Making him spur the crowd on. The hell dog had been blind drunk on the hate that spilled from these ordinary people. He had danced around them, whispering in their ears, feeding on the anger. They had left as the police arrived. A manipulated community had been put into vans, puzzled at why they were even there, not even knowing what they had said. The family had had children. Terrified.

Frightened to let go of the parents who had had to run to escape, to hide behind that locked door, and to hope that the authorities would come quick enough.

Danny was ashamed. He couldn't fight him. He wasn't strong enough. He thought of Lucy again, and wondered what she was doing. Whether his mum had come back to her. How long had it been, anyway? He wasn't sure. It felt like weeks, but then, he hadn't eaten, so it couldn't have been too long. He wouldn't have survived. Or would he? This creature who had absolute power over him was obviously not of this world. Who knew what he could do with time? Danny shook his head to try and release his thoughts, but they just could not escape the black net they were trapped in.

Gwyllgi rose to his feet, flung back his head and howled into the night.

"It's time to call my followers," he said. "Let's see what havoc they've managed, shall we?" He laughed again, the gruff sound echoing around the field where they'd stopped to rest. Danny's skin crawled with the feeling of the howl. It was the sound of a thousand screams all at once, scratching at the dark sky. At once there was an answer, screeches far away in the dusk.

"They will follow," he said. "And now to move on. We cannot be still."

Danny had no idea where they were, or where they had been. The village they had visited was unrecognisable to him. It could have been anywhere. He had noticed that the houses looked different, not the yellowy stone he was used to in their village, but flint with red window surrounds, and squat roofs of red slate. They must have travelled far, but he knew not where. With his head so fuzzy, he could barely tell whether it was morning or night, let alone their location. It was all he could do to hold Lucy in his mind. His weird and wonderful little sister, with her scruffy hair and baggy t-shirts. He tried to remember her voice, that sweet and clear sound, so unfiltered. He closed his eyes and concentrated. Just one memory of that sound. Anything. But it would not come to him. Danny's eyes started to feel watery. He felt so foolish.

26

The Finding

Puck was standing under the Yew, his thin arm reaching up to the broken branch, checking it to see how it had healed.

"Good evening, Lucy," he said, solemnly bowing. "I am so sorry it has come to this."

"Where is the Council?" Ceinwen's eyes burned into him this time. Puck's shoulders seemed to sink, and his hooded eyes looked to the ground.

"They have refused us help." The pain was clear on his face. "They say that one human is a satisfactory loss in what is becoming a war." He took a few steps towards them and held out his palms. "I am so sorry, Lucy. We are on our own, but I do not hold out much hope. Even with the three of us working together, I fear that it will not be enough."

Ceinwen's cheeks flushed with anger. Fists balled, she batted him away. "Well, you shoulda persuaded them."

"I spent several hours with the leaders, but they said that their priorities lay elsewhere. That the Black Dog's power was greatly reduced over these years."

"Greatly reduced? GREATLY REDUCED!" Ceinwen turned away, muttering into the wind. The breeze around them started to swirl with mist, and icy particles stabbed Lucy's skin. The muttering was in the old language, and Lucy found that she understood exactly what the words were, and they were not repeatable.

"Ceinwen, be calm. I tried my best. We are on our own. We will just have to accept it."

Lucy's cheeks reddened, too. "But why? What about the meeting? I thought I'd helped."

"I thought so too, Lucy, but it seems that several villages in the north have been attacked by three spirit-hounds, causing all sorts of mayhem. They say they must investigate. Danny must wait."

Ceinwen turned towards them, her hair wild and her skin glowing. Her eyes were darker than usual, like a raging ocean rather than a calm pond. "But don't they understand that it is likely to be Gwyllgi and his followers? They underestimate his influence. AH! They are idiots." She flung her hands into the air and the mist immediately dissipated, falling to the earth and disappearing.

"I also feel there is a connection, but unfortunately, the Council is young. They don't remember him as we do. They only know the stories, and I'm sure you are aware how they have been diluted over the years."

Ceinwen sighed heavily. "Well, we must do as we can. Let's at least try'n locate Danny." She held her hands out. Puck took one and held his other hand out to Lucy.

"Might I suggest, given your power, that you remove your shoes?" Puck looked down at Lucy's sodden trainers.

"Oh. Right." She reached down and pulled them off at the heel. Shoving her socks into them, her toes tingled as soon as they touched the moist grass.

"Join hands with us, Lucy. Close your eyes and visualise Danny. We will give you our strength. Tell us what you see." Puck's fingers wrapped around Lucy's palm, slender but strong, warm against her own chilled skin. Ceinwen held her other hand. Hers was rough. A farmer's hands, tough, but gentle.

"Ready?" she said.

"I suppose. I'm not sure."

"We'll protect you. We won't let go. Promise."

Lucy took a deep breath and closed her eyes.

Immediately, her mind picture formed, covering a few metres around her. She started humming, almost without thinking, and the picture spread to the edge of the meadow. She saw ghost versions of her mum and grandma sitting motionless on the sofa. Eyes closed, arms resting, breathing steadily, a serene look on both faces. They were safe. Then she felt a warmth spreading into her palms and up to her elbows, gradually filling her veins with a wonderful glow. She gasped, but the mind picture that only extended out when she hummed remained where it was.

"Go further." She heard Puck's voice emanate from somewhere inside her head. "We will help you."

Lucy had to make a conscious effort to accept the power travelling up her arms and inwards into her body. Her mind was trying to protect her from the strange sensation. She had to trust it, trust Ceinwen and Puck. Trust that they knew what they were doing. She breathed through it, letting the heat, almost unbearable now, spread through her body and into her lungs. She took a deep breath and let out a long steady note. Not just a quiet humming through her lips, but a call. Out into the air around her.

As she sang, her mind picture spread out so far it was as if she was flying. Up, up into the sky, floating above

175

the Yew, like a balloon on a long string. She was looking down onto the meadow and saw a circle of three people holding hands. She looked out and across. She could see all four coasts from the white cliffs of Dover, to the high, clean sea spray at Land's End, to the scattered islands off the far north of Scotland. Everything in between was there, all contained in one picture. She could see it as a whole, but also focus on one part, any part she liked, any detail she desired.

She saw the glow of London and felt the deep chatter of a million people. City traffic, thick polluted air and constant bustle. She looked out towards the southwest. There was a glimpse of great power coming from a ring of stones. A column of light stretched up from them and disappeared into the dusk. Stonehenge, she realised, remembering a holiday when she was little. Up to the north and the cold metal of an angel, silhouetted against an orange sky. It was raining there, and she could feel the individual drops as they spat onto the angel and then splintered out into the air, making a halo of mist.

She could feel the thrum of each droplet against her skin, the vibrations of a billion living things, held in her pores. She could see everything.

Danny.

She remembered why she was here. Think of Danny, they had said. In that moment her brain seemed to focus on the word, which then formed an image of him. Huddled under a hedge, pale and shivering. His eyes were black, and she felt a deep sorrow. It was him. She had found him. She searched around, trying to see a landmark that would give some clue. She needed more time, but her breath was running out. She forced the air from her lungs, her stomach hurting with the effort to extend the sound that was coming from her throat. Just a couple more seconds.

Then she saw him.

The dog. The monster. His shape was so dark it overpowered her. The creature turned, and Lucy saw the death in his eyes. Heard him snarl. With that, she fell. Back to the meadow. When she opened her eyes, she was lying on the soft grass. Puck and Ceinwen were there beside her, nudging her gently to wake her. Her eyes were sticky as she opened them. The warmth had gone. Her chest and throat stung.

"I know where he is," she said.

27

The Chase

Ceinwen retrieved a battered thermos flask from what must have been a very deep coat pocket.

"Here, drink this." She loosened the top and poured some strong-smelling tea. Lucy recognised it from that first night at the cottage. It seemed weeks ago, but was merely two days. Such a lot had happened in such a short time. The hours seemed to have stretched into a lifetime. Lucy breathed in the steam and felt immediately better. Goodness knows what was in this stuff, but it was good. She let the warm liquid run down her throat and into her stomach, and a calm feeling took over. The blanket was on the ground, and she pulled it up over her shoulders again.

"So?"

"I saw the monster, and Danny was with him. He had black eyes and looked really scared."

Ceinwen sat beside her on the grass. Lucy took another sip.

"Where are they?"

Lucy wrapped her hands around the flask top and looked into the tea. There was a storm cloud of green sediment swirling at the bottom.

"They were near the metal angel, a few miles away. You know, the big statue."

"I KNEW IT! I knew he was in the north." Ceinwen slapped the ground with her hand and stood up.

"We must move quickly, or we'll lose 'im."

"Wait!" Puck rose from the ground. "Remember, it's only us. The Council has abandoned us. We need a plan."

He offered a hand to Lucy, which she took. With a strength far greater than Lucy expected from such a small person, he pulled her to standing. For the first time Lucy saw some of his great age showing in the deep grey of his eyes.

"We can't just go in and attack. Only we know how powerful Gwyllgi really is." In his face was the pain of a previous memory.

Ceinwen paced, rubbing her wrist.

"We'll have to hide. Go into our animal shapes. Well, Lucy and me. Can you manage, Puck?"

"I have a way."

"Lucy, you'll need to change again. Can you do it? Have you enough energy?"

"I think so." Lucy wrapped the blanket tighter around her, remembering how it became part of her.

"Then we go. Could you see the area around where they were? Could you get us a little way away? Maybe half a mile?"

Lucy nodded.

"OK. Once we get close, you MUST hide, Lucy, do you hear me? You must leave it to Puck and me. OK? You have the blanket. You will be safe as long as you have it. You must stay away from him, he is too dangerous."

The weight of what they were about to do sat heavily in Lucy's chest. Running towards something that frightened her was not something that Lucy was good at. Quite the opposite. But this was Danny. Poor Danny, trapped by that evil creature. Not able to escape, having to do what it said. In her mind, she made a decision. Resolved her thoughts. This time she would run towards the problem, not away. Fight, not flight. Closing her eyes, she had a firm picture of him in her head. Clear, and full colour, resonating as if the picture itself had the power to bring him back. This was what she was here for. She would get Puck and Ceinwen to him. They could do this.

"All right. I'm ready."

Puck nodded to Ceinwen, and they held out their hands.

Lucy felt the warmth quicker this time. She instinctively knew to let it in, let it flow through her. This time when she sang, she knew where to look. In just a moment she had found Danny and then looked nearby for a safe place. There was a derelict barn two fields away from him. Ceinwen sensed that she had found somewhere and started muttering under her breath. The words danced from her lips and joined with Lucy's note, combining into a melody, like a singer harmonising with a fiddle player. The words seemed to just fit. A mist appeared from nowhere and surrounded them, spinning faster and faster until Lucy felt her feet lift from the ground.

"Keep the place in your mind, Lucy. Concentrate." Puck's voice floated into her head again.

The mist swirled and Lucy felt herself lift up and up. It was different from before. When she flew before she knew it was just her thoughts with her feet firmly placed in the grass of the meadow, her toes gripping the dirt. This time she felt the weight of her body come with her, and cold air swathed her soles, making them tingle. She felt Ceinwen's and Puck's hands gripping onto hers. They were doing it together. Before she knew it, her feet touched earth again and she smelled the dust and wood of an old building. She opened her eyes and saw wooden walls and a corrugated roof. Grey sky peered through the holes. A light rain pattered, leaking through onto her hair, and she stopped singing.

"Well done, Lucy." Ceinwen smiled at her. "You really are the most powerful human I have ever met."

"We must move quickly." Puck peered through a gap where the old door had fallen half off its hinges.

"They're that way." Lucy pointed out and over the adjacent fields. Ceinwen looked out and nodded.

"Right. Lucy, you must stay out of sight. We will change into our animal forms. Keep an eye out for rabbit holes. They're good hiding places in an emergency."

Lucy nodded. Ceinwen had already started to transform, so Lucy closed her eyes, stuck her fingers in her ears and thought, 'mole'. Her skin felt tight and her nose itched, but in moments she was small, black and furry again, proud that she could do it with no help after so little time. Puck, meanwhile, had disappeared.

"Where's Puck?" she asked, glancing around. Her eyesight as a mole wasn't great. She could still sense him, but he was gone.

"I'm here." The air in front of them shifted, and Lucy realised that Puck was indeed still standing in front of her, but his body had changed. He was every shade of green and brown, leaf shapes and twigs, bits of barn and sky. His whole body was changing to match what was behind him. Not invisible, exactly, but just blending in, as though the fields around him had just lent him a matching jacket and trousers. He had pulled a hood and scarf around his face so that only his eyes were floating in mid-air.

"Don't look so surprised, Lucy-mole! You have your skills, I have mine." He smiled briefly. "Light is my specialty. It does what I want and reflects what I want."

"Stop showin' off, Sprite. We've got work to do."

Ceinwen bounded out of the barn door and off across the field, tail bobbing. Puck exchanged a look with Lucy, who then lolloped after her, her small legs struggling to keep any decent pace. Puck was beside her, the light rain bouncing lightly off him and creating a sparkling halo around him. Lucy might have been powerful, but she was in the presence of two very powerful beings in their own right, and she suddenly felt overwhelmingly privileged to be allowed into their world.

28

The Fight

As they crept along the hedge of the last field, Lucy had a heavy feeling that she couldn't shake. There was a dank smell emanating from the ground and every paw print in the soil made her more nauseated. The closer they got to the creature, the blacker the earth became. Carcasses of insects littered their path where the creatures hadn't had time to flee from the encroaching rot.

Then they saw them.

Danny was sitting on the grass with his head on his knees, clothes wet and dirty and hair plastered to his head from the rain. He was so much smaller than Lucy remembered. The monster was almost serene next to him, licking its yellow claws, seemingly oblivious to their approach.

There was a small hollow in the earth by a hawthorn trunk. Ceinwen signalled to Lucy to duck down and stay put, and then with a quick nod to Puck she scampered on silent hare feet along the hedge to the far end of the field. Puck took a deep breath and straightened up, stepping out towards Gwyllgi and his prisoner.

"Ah, Puck, what a privilege! Not brought your Council friends with you, then?" The creature's chuckle was as a knife through sand.

"Give me the human." Puck strode towards them, hands out in front of him. He had thrown off his natural disguise now, melting his form back into being. Risking everything to ensure the Black Dog was looking only at him. The creature laughed louder and threw his head back. Blood soaked teeth dripped and spattered onto the blackened grass around him.

"Whyever would I do that? He's been quite the little helper, haven't you, Danny?"

Danny raised his head a little, looking at Puck with his black eyes. His lips parted as he attempted the words, 'help me', but it was too difficult. His forehead lolled onto his knees again. Lucy's heart felt as if it wanted to wrench clean out of her chest. It was taking all her strength to stay quiet and safe.

"What would you want with one of these weaklings, anyway? They're only good for puppetry." Gwyllgi rose to his feet. At full height, he was twice that of Puck, and yet the sprite did not slow his approach. "Give me the human," he repeated as he rose his hands up, conjuring a small light from his fingertips which rolled around his palms threateningly.

"You have no Council to help you this time, Puck. Are they scared of a great beast such as me? Are they cowering in that cave of theirs? Oh, yes, I know about that little hiding place. I'll get to it eventually. What are you going to do? Give me some light to read by?" A menacing growl sounded in his throat, like distant thunder.

Puck glanced to his left as a fully-formed Ceinwen strode out towards Gwyllgi. From her palm she blew a cloud of grey dust, and then immediately made a mist that streamed out, carrying the dust around the feet of the great dog. It curled and rolled, licking at the ground and stretching tendrils through the thick fur, covering the bare bone patches with its swirling cloak. Puck leaped forward and shone a bright beam into Gwyllgi's eyes.

There was a roar so loud that it cracked the trunk of the hawthorn, and Lucy could only try to cover her mole ears with her paws. The sound pulsed through her, making her fur spike, while the wood splintered onto her back. She shifted away from the debris, out a little into the field. She knew she was breaking cover, but just avoided a falling branch whose leaves were blackening even as it fell. Meanwhile Ceinwen had surrounded the beast with her mist, and the spores she had sent to create a trap were growing rapidly into grey domes. Gwyllgi turned his head from the light and blindly stepped back. His great paw slammed into the ground and he snarled. Teeth bared, he reached out to Danny and plunged his head to the ground, full weight upon him, his claws around his neck. Danny could do nothing but scratch at the soil and look bleakly into the creatures dripping snout.

"DANNY! NO!" Lucy's scream was out before she knew it. Puck and Ceinwen were thrown back onto the ground and the mushrooms pulsed with a blue grey light. Insects, spiders, and beetles were rising in waves all around her, rushing to their deaths to protect her. In Lucy's horror she saw her brother's body was stretched across the line of mushrooms, clearly creating some sort of bridge between the inside of the rapidly growing fairy circle and freedom. Gwyllgi twisted and burned his eyes into Lucy before releasing Danny and striding across him towards Lucy's hiding place, batting away Lucy's miniature army with one disdainful paw. Danny coughed in air and grabbed his neck, wheezing.

"Well, well, well, what do we have here?" The dog's huge feet were padding towards her. The pads were pushing into the soil in slow motion, invading the ground with each step, blackness spreading like a carpet in his wake. Lucy was frozen with dread. She had shown him what she could do. He wanted her, and her only.

Puck and Ceinwen scrabbled desperately to stand, breaking into a run, feet hardly touching the ground. Ceinwen was surprisingly quick, pounding her legs. Puck leaping in great strides, covering ground enough for a giant. They dived under the hedge to meet her, and in the split second their hands were on her, Lucy thought, *meadow*. Ceinwen's mist surrounded them, uttering the old words as quickly as she could. Then the words cut short as she screamed. The beast had embedded his claws into her back, and her face contorted.

The air rushed past them as the three rose up. Lucy's body returned as they flew, and they landed heavily on the grass by the Yew. The blanket splayed out under her onto the wet grass. It had taken all Ceinwen's strength to return them to safety, but as she sprawled forward onto the ground, they could see the long black marks cut clear through her coat and clothes to her skin. Thick blood seeped out. They were not deep, but the skin was red and sore. The dog's claws had introduced their rot into the wound. She was poisoned.

29

The Song

"He will follow. Quick, get her into the cottage." The rain had started spitting here, too. It was dark now, and the only light was a dim reflection from the moon on tumbling clouds. Puck and Lucy took Ceinwen's arms and lifted her to sitting. She was awake but unresponsive, eyes starting to grey already. She was so heavy. Even with Puck's unexpected strength, his height made it difficult to get her to standing. In the end, they pulled her to lean awkwardly against the Yew, huddled in her ripped raincoat still.

"I'll get some of the healing moss. Wait with her."

But no sooner had Puck stepped away than they felt a low rumble. Puck halted on the hill, and Lucy's breath caught in her throat as she felt the meadow under her shudder. The unseen creatures were scrambling to get away, and Lucy could hear their distress. There before them was the great Black Dog, with Danny lying limp between its front legs. There was nothing they could do. At full strength, Puck and Ceinwen had failed to trap the beast. It was hopeless now that Ceinwen was injured.

Gwyllgi launched up onto his hind legs, slammed his claws into the ground and roared again. Spittle flew from his grey lips, and the green mist that was settled in his throat seeped out at his fangs. He could feel that the Sentinel and its guardian were weak, and he would not be wasting the moment.

Lucy heard a horrendous crack. Ceinwen cried out from her stupor as the Yew shook and split down its centre. The yellow wood splayed, and the branches parted, falling away to earth. Puck and Lucy grabbed Ceinwen again, and despite her complaints, dragged her a short way from the tree, just avoiding a falling bough. Out in the meadow, the rings of mushrooms were glowing and pulsing. The fairy circles were failing, and Gwyllgi's compatriots would soon swarm out into the world.

In desperation, Lucy flung the blanket over Ceinwen in the hope that it would give her protection. This was all too much, and the familiar ball of rage in her stomach was growing. Her brain was telling her to run. Get away. Escape.

On her knees, she started to rock and hum. The familiar movements had comforted her since she was a toddler. She wanted to scream, but her body was in shock, she couldn't do it. Back and forth, back and forth, back and forth. The hum was louder in her throat now. She opened her mouth and the sound became fuller. Closing her eyes to shut out the monster, she covered her ears with her hands and rocked harder. Back and forth, back and forth, back and forth. Just then she felt a hand on her shoulder, firm and warm, despite her injury. Ceinwen had stirred. Lucy opened her eyes and looked into the old woman's. Despite the grey there was a glimmer of light. Then Lucy began to hear music, familiar and old. Ceinwen was looking intently at her, silently sending the words to her. The old language filled her throat and Lucy found herself mouthing the words of a lullaby she was sure she had heard a million times, but from a past life which wasn't her own.

> *Huna blentyn ar fy mynwes*
> *Clyd a chynnes ydyw hon;*
> *Breichiau mam sy'n dynn amdanat,*
> *Cariad mam sy dan fy mron.*
> *Ni chaiff dim amharu'th gyntun,*
> *Ni wna undyn â thi gam;*

Huna'n dawel, annwyl blentyn,
Huna'n fwyn ar fron dy fam.

There was a picture forming in her mind, not of the meadow, but from the past. A dark-haired woman in a chair by a fire, rocking a baby wrapped in a green blanket with square patterns. Lucy knew instantly what to do. Digging her hand deep into her pocket, her fingers wrapped around the cherry stone. It was warm from her body heat and damp from the rain that had soaked her jeans. She pushed herself to her feet and lunged forward towards the creature. Plunging the seed into the ground, her knuckles hit tiny stones and stray roots and pushed them aside. Her palm pressed the seed deep into the sodden earth, and she held it down. She dug her toes into the mud, closed her eyes and sang, sang as loud as she could.

The lullaby that mother had sung to her child, the words that sung themselves into the blanket and into the Sentinel Cherry that guarded her home, the magic that had woven itself into her, bled down into the ground through her fingers. While her lips formed the words, her mind reached into the soil, willing the seed to grow, begging the meadow to help her. In her head the mind picture grew, and she sensed a thousand creatures, a million insects and a billion roots and their buried lives turn towards them. They had heard her.

Puck gasped as he felt the energy pour through the ground. He, too, knelt and offered himself through the earth, palms down and eyes closed. Everything he had, he pushed towards the cherry stone, sensing it writhe and vibrate from metres away.

Gwyllgi rose to his hind legs once more, but his roar was silent against the weight of the song. When his feet beat at the ground, they were soundless this time. Danny convulsed, his chest raised upwards, his hands grasping at the earth. His eyes were no longer black, and he knew he was free of the beast. He dragged himself up and forced his legs to move away. His limbs were weak, and his energy spent, but he could see Lucy. His little Lucy. Mud soaking his clothes and spattering his face, he crawled away from the monster that had kept his mind prisoner and used him so repulsively for hate. There she was, reaching into the ground and singing, and there was a halo of light around her. The air around him vibrated, and he knew it was Lucy making it happen.

Enraged that he no longer had power over Danny, Gwyllgi lashed out, narrowly missing him. Danny rose and half walked, half crawled to Lucy. He looked on in awe as a sapling snaked from the ground, lashing and writhing towards the sky, its leaves growing and spinning in high speed. He looked at the creature and he was filled with hate. What this creature had made him do disgusted him. He looked around for a weapon and saw a fragment from the Yew. The wood was still yellow and fresh from the destruction of the tree, and Danny felt heavy with the memory that he had taken his anger out on that beautiful tree that had done nothing to deserve it. The hell hound had taken advantage of him in a time of pain, using his guilt and anger to gain control over him. But that's it, he thought. Anger would not defeat this creature. He needed to rid himself of it.

He picked it up and weighed it in his hands. It was jagged and it pushed tiny splinters into his palm as he gripped it, but he did not feel them. It was Lucy who had found him, and Lucy who needed him now. He could hear her voice, the one that, until now, had only been for him. That voice, the crystal-clear tones... She was using her own beauty, her own legacy to fight. In that moment, his mind was clear. He listened to Lucy's melody and let it take over him. Let the love he had for his sister overtake the hate.

The dog was raising itself up again, feet dancing to avoid the Cherry's writhing stalks, pawing at the air. Its head was lolling from side to side, pained with the song that was enslaving it. Without a sound, and with his heart filled with music, Danny rushed at the dog and plunged the Yew branch deep into its chest. The branch glowed and spat against the matted fur and the creature bared its teeth, silenced, but still just as terrifying. The rain pelted them, and the meadow was covered in rivulets of water, each trickle like a million tiny bells. The Cherry sapling had now wrapped itself around the shoulders of Gwyllgi, squeezing him tight as he squirmed in pain. Danny scrambled away to Lucy.

Puck looked around at the circles, and saw they were no longer glowing red, but were pulsing with a blue light. The barriers were strengthening as the new Cherry grew. The sapling was becoming a trunk, the width of a woman's wrist, and then a leg, and then as thick as Lucy's waist. All the time twisting and squeezing, snaking and spiralling. As it touched the impaled Yew branch it seemed to quicken, and the whole squirming mass was bathed in light.

30

The Trap

The rain was plummeting to the ground in rods, soaking everything within seconds and creating streams of mud. Debris from the obliterated Yew was floating away, while miniature waterfalls passed over the larger branches that could not be lifted. The clouds were low and grey, and rolled into themselves as they tumbled across the sky.

The only light now was that which shone from the meadow's new Sentinel as its growth slowed, encasing Gwyllgi completely. Puck was next to Ceinwen, who was crying silently. Her Yew had gone. Her heart felt as if it had split down its centre along with the trunk. Lucy and Danny sat close to each other, neither caring that they were soaked through and sitting in a mud puddle. Danny's arm was around Lucy's shoulders, and she could feel the warmth of him on her bare neck. Before them was the most magnificent Cherry tree, much larger than any they had ever seen, and in full blossom. The branches were youthful and strong, with muscle-like bulges stretching their length. The bark was smooth, as yet untouched by the elements, and the central trunk was arrow straight. The rain that was making every blade of grass bow down with pressure was not even touching it, and the petals flourished as if it were a calm, sunny day.

Within a few moments, the rain stopped, the sky cleared, and it was full of stars. The fresh scent of the blossom wafted over them, as if to say, 'It's over, rest now.' The sound of running water was everywhere as the rain found its lowest point and flowed down the incline away from them, each rivulet reflecting its own family of stars from above.

Danny stood up, offering a hand to Lucy.

"You are the most amazing woman I will ever know." He smiled, and gave her a bear hug, which Lucy melted into without a pause or a flinch. "Thank you. You just saved my life, little sis."

"We have to help Ceinwen. She's injured." Lucy broke away and walked to where Puck was kneeling. Ceinwen was pale and shivering, but as Lucy approached, she smiled.

"Well done, Lucy. You're a guardian now. And such a beautiful Sentinel tree." Her skin was still grey, but her eyes were bright again.

"I had no idea I could do that. It just came to me. I had the Cherry stone in my pocket and…" Lucy had a sudden thought that she must thank the mother Cherry at the cottage. Thank her for providing a child to grow and protect the meadow.

"You have done well." Puck rose to shake her hand, bowing as he did so. "You are a very special person, Lucy." His face fell a little and looked sorrowful. "Although you do realise that this is your tree now, don't you? This is your Sentinel. You will need to stay nearby."

Lucy thought carefully and realised that this was something she didn't mind. She felt a connection with this meadow now. Maybe she would be here in another hundred and fifty years, an old woman like Ceinwen, protecting the world from the evil that only she knew was trapped here. It was one of the most terrifying things, to have that much responsibility, but somehow it seemed like this was what

Lucy was waiting for. Like it was something she was always meant to do. She looked down at the hand she had given to Puck. He still held it gently, and Lucy could feel her fingers tingling. On her fourth finger was a plain silver band. It glowed softly in the light of the new Sentinel. She thought of the ring she had seen on Ceinwen's hand only a few days before. Ceinwen seemed to know what she was thinking and held up her hand to show her own ring. It was still there, but much thinner. The surface was dull and pitted.

"I still have the Apple," she said. "Speaking of which, I could do with one of those apples right now. Together with a cup of tea. We have a lot to discuss, Lucy."

Together they helped Ceinwen hobble to her cottage.

"I never knew this cottage was here." Danny wondered at the Apple tree, weighed down with fruit at completely the wrong time of year. "How on earth are these growing now?" He picked at a large red one at head height. This one was clear of holes, freshly grown and blemish free.

"After everything that's happened over the last few days, you're most surprised about the apples?" Ceinwen chuckled. "Hand it over. My need is greater than yours…" Danny did so without hesitation. He bowed and offered it from the palm of his hand.

"M'Lady."

"Watch it, boy." But there was a smile in Ceinwen's eyes. She already liked him.

As they entered the cottage a sudden exhaustion overcame Lucy, and she could see that Danny was about to collapse, too.

"Have you got any of that magic tea?" she asked.

"I know where to find it." Puck started rummaging for a teapot. "I think you need to hand over your recipe, Ceinwen."

"One thing at a time, Sprite. One thing at a time!"

It seemed that Ceinwen's injuries weren't as bad as they'd first thought. As soon as Gwyllgi became trapped in the Sentinel, the infection receded, and they were mere scratches. A good packing of the dry moss that seemed to be in abundance in the cottage pantry soothed them immediately. By the time tea had been sipped, and apples crunched, the four were ready to part ways. The sky was starting to lighten to a blue grey and a fresh sunrise shone over a rain-soaked meadow.

"I think I'd better go and face the music." Danny stood and offered a hand to both Puck and Ceinwen in turn.

"I cannot thank you enough for your help, and once again, I am so sorry about the Yew."

"What music?" Ceinwen and Lucy said aloud in unison. Puck and Danny erupted in laughter.

"Like peas in a pod, you two! Yes, Danny, you'd better go and see how your mother is. Got your story straight?"

"I think so. Come on, Luce."

Lucy's shoes were long gone, carried away on some river of soil and muck. She squelched down the hill with Danny towards the cottage, twiddling the ring with her thumb and glowing inside from what she had done.

Little Lucy. The weird one. The one who couldn't fit in. The one who was 'special', but not in a good way. Lucy had saved the world with powers she never knew she had. With each step she sensed the world under her feet. The sounds of nature were next to her ears, the smells that she loved, the feel of the early morning. This was her meadow now. She was this way for a reason. She was here for a reason. And she would remain here, for a reason.

31

The Flood

As they walked down Lucy's path towards the back door of the cottage, they heard a shriek. Lucy exchanged a glance with Danny before rushing to open the door.

As they entered the kitchen, Lucy realised that her feet were still wet. The floor was covered with a shallow pool of muddy water.

"What on EARTH…" Grandma's voice sang out from the living room.

The entire downstairs of the house was flooded, and Mum and Grandma had woken to find the cold water lapping at their toes. Lucy entered to find them confused and tired, kneeling on the sofa, looking incredulously at the carpet, which was rippling sedately.

"Er, you, er, must have fallen asleep on the sofa?" Lucy volunteered. "I, I came back and went straight to bed. I've been here all the time, honest!"

Mum looked at her suspiciously and was just about to probe further into Lucy's obviously unreliable statement, when she heard the front door slam.

"Danny?"

He had closed the door to make it seem like he had just got back, and sheepishly stepped into the living room.

"DANNY!" Mum leaped from the sofa and rushed to him, not caring about the waves and splashes as she waded towards him.

"Where have you been, young man? Your mother has been worried sick!" Grandma was up on her feet with her hands on her hips. She did not look pleased.

"Not now, Mum, he's back, and that's what matters."

"But you called the police and everything!" She turned to Danny with a wagging finger. "You need to explain yourself."

"I'm so sorry, Mum, Grandma," Danny hugged Mum tight. "I was so angry I just kept walking. After a few hours I got lost and spent the night under a hedge."

Lucy knew that this wasn't entirely a lie. She tried to look surprised and pleased that Danny was back, but it was difficult to show on her face when the truth was that she had been at his side for hours.

"I lost my phone and my wallet. It's taken me this long to get home. I'm so sorry, I didn't mean to worry you…and I DEFINITELY did not mean to leave Lucy on her own. The time just ran away. I really am sorry." He looked at Lucy. She could see that his apology was directed at her. Despite everything, he wanted to make it clear that he had not deserted her. Lucy was not one for the attention to be on her and would normally have changed the subject very quickly, but after all that had happened it felt right to take his hand and give it a squeeze.

"I know," she said.

"It's OK, Danny, it's OK. You're home. You're safe. That's what matters." Mum hugged him again and seemed so happy. She didn't care that her trousers had a muddy tide mark, and that her very expensive sofa was ruined. And she seemed to have forgotten that she'd spent the entire night sitting on the sofa completely unaware that her home was silently filling with water. She just knew that Danny and Lucy were safe, and that was what was important. She looked strangely calm, as though she'd merely woken from a really good night's sleep.

"I'll call that police officer in a while. I'm pretty sure they weren't actively doing anything anyway."

Grandma's face softened, and after a moment's confusion she said,

"Well, we best not use the electricity, but I'm sure I can improvise a cup of tea from a pan on the gas cooker." Off she waded, tutting at the carpet, and the muddy splashes on the wallpaper.

"Should we be letting Grandma do that?" Lucy said. And as if nothing had happened, they all headed to the kitchen to see what the damage was, and whether a cup of tea was feasible after all.

They had managed to persuade Grandma not to turn on the oven, under the circumstances. Mum was rummaging around under the stairs for a mop. Danny had walked a circuit of the house to see what the damage was and had managed to improvise 'sandbags' out of some supermarket carrier bags and soil from higher up the garden. He was trying to create a low barrier by the front door when a Land Rover pulled up on the roadside. A man in a wax jacket and with particularly hairy earlobes got out of the driver's seat, and from the passenger side stepped a woman with the most spectacular black curly hair and sporting bright orange wellies.

"Ahoy, there!" called the man, wading over to Danny. "Dr Cooke...Jim. This is my friend's daughter, Elizabeth. Just checking around the village to see if everyone's OK. Bit of a shock, this flood. Caught everyone by surprise. Nothing in the forecast. Nothing!" He threw his hands in the air and shook his head as if the floods were entirely the weatherman's fault. He was well spoken, and had a moustache which wiggled enthusiastically, like a tiny ferret. Elizabeth offered a hand to Danny.

"Hiya. Not met you yet. My Mums run the pub. The Hare?"

"Oh, hi, Elizabeth. Erm, I'm Danny. Did you say Mums?"

"Yeah, I've got two. I'm greedy like that. You got enough sandbags?"

"Well, we haven't got any, but these seem to work OK. Temporarily at least. I thought it was just us. Is the village flooded, too?"

Dr Cooke bent down to give him a hand filling another bag. "We've called on nine houses so far and they've all got some water ingress. The pub is OK, they're further up the hill. The surgery has a few steps up to the door, so that's survived, thank goodness." He raised his eyes to the sky and sighed deeply with relief. "The Post Office has had a few inches, but thankfully all their shelves are off the floor. It'll be a job to clear it, though, as they'll have to heft everything out to change the carpet. It's mostly the residents, I think."

"Crikey, I didn't realise." In his head, Danny silently noted that this was all his fault, although he could never reveal why. It was a secret he would have to keep to himself. "Can I help?"

Elizabeth pinched a bit of Danny's jumper between her fingers. "Maybe you ought to change your clothes first? You're soaked!"

Danny had completely forgotten. He must have looked a sight with his unwashed hair and filthy jeans. Elizabeth chuckled, and it sounded like water over pebbles. Danny noticed that she had green eyes, which were so bright against her caramel skin.

"Er… Yeah. Probably should. Er, maybe I'll finish here and then go and see if the post office needs anything doing."

At that moment, Mum poked her head out of the kitchen window. "Dr Cooke! How simply lovely to see you!" She was using the posh voice again. "I would offer you tea, but we're not switching anything on, just in case. You don't know a good electrician, do you?"

"That I do, Ms Chatham, that I do." He got out an ancient phone and relayed a phone number through the open window, holding it at arm's length because he'd 'forgotten those damn specs again.'

"Hang on, I need something to write on." Mum scrabbled around the kitchen to find her phone, or a scrap of paper.

Lucy, who was at the kitchen table, legs crossed so her feet didn't get wet, reached into her back pocket and drew out the packet of Post-it Notes and the holiday pen. The paper was a little wrinkled and damp but had survived surprisingly well.

"Here you go, Mum." She held them out to her.

Mum looked at them as though Lucy had offered to chop off her head for her. "Are you sure, love? I know you like to keep those close to you."

Lucy smiled. "It's OK. I don't need them anymore." She turned back to the book she was reading and wiggled her bare toes against her jeans. Mum smiled the biggest smile she had for a long time.

"OK, Luce. Thank you. Thank you so much."

Elizabeth poked Danny on the arm. "So Mum Saffy is going to put on a big chilli at the pub tonight. Thought we'd feed the village until the electricity gets checked out. You coming? I'll expect a better outfit, though." She winked at him and looked pointedly at his mud-caked trainers.

Danny smiled. "Yeah. That would be good! Why not? I'll bring the folks. I'm sure they'll appreciate it."

"See you then."

"See you later."

He watched as Elizabeth jumped lightly back into the passenger seat next to 'Jim', and had a strange feeling that he would be seeing her rather a lot.

32

The Hare

The day had been busy, but Lucy and Danny had never met so many people in the village in just a few hours. Everyone had pulled together, making sure all the residents were safe, helping those who needed it and offering showers, sandwiches and endless cups of tea to those who'd been affected by the flash flood. There had even been a brief visit from a TV company, asking questions about the localised storm and speculating why the MET office hadn't predicted it. Dr Cooke said it was his 'five minutes of fame', as he answered a question about how the community had all 'come together' to help. Although he still hadn't located his glasses.

That evening, the Chatham family walked the mile and a bit to a wonky brick building with ivy covering the gable end. The sign jutting from under the eaves rocked gently back and forth and pictured a majestic-looking Hare, front paws out in readiness to leap, and with bright, mustard yellow eyes.

"Apparently it's been called the Hare for over a hundred years. Local tradition." Mum rummaged in her handbag to check she had her purse while Lucy stared into the eyes of the painting and wondered if, all those years ago, it had been based on one particular hare.

They opened the door to a bustling room filled with tables, scraping chairs and loud chatting. Bouts of booming laughter and shouts of greeting were muffled by the low beams. The smell of the smoke from the wood fire mixed with chilli and beer, intensified by the heat from many bodies. Lucy froze in the doorway. There were too many people. There were too many smells, too many sounds. She'd had too little sleep and her worry bucket was already full. Her chest felt tight and she just felt a wave of huge disappointment wash over her. She was desperate to go in, but her feet wouldn't move. They were trapped inside her wellies, with three pairs of socks, but she was longing to take them off and ground herself.

"You OK, Lucy?" Danny stayed by her side as Mum and Grandma were engulfed by the throng, cheerfully commenting on how 'nice' it was to meet everybody, their voices combining so naturally with the crowd.

Lucy couldn't speak. She froze and felt that familiar creeping feeling of wanting to escape. To run. Her heart was beating against her chest and her skin prickled against her jumper sleeves. After all that had happened. After all that bravery she had in her when it was important. And now this. The same old Lucy, frightened to enter a noisy room. Why did she have to be this way?

Just then, a bouncing mess of curly black hair made its way through the tables.

"Hiya, Lucy. Bit loud in this room. Wanna come round to the back? There's a great little nook behind the fireplace." Lucy nodded, unable to respond. Elizabeth took her hand and led her quickly through the tables and around the side of the bar. The space was quieter, but Lucy could still see Mum from a distance, gleefully patting Dr Cooke on the arm and swilling a glass of red wine. The wall of the fireplace muted the sound from the front room, and as Danny pulled out a chair the legs were silent against the oatmeal-coloured carpet.

"Better?" Elizabeth poked at the fire and added a log from a huge wicker basket. "This is Mum Jo's favourite

214

place to sit and do the accounts. Let's just say I have a radar for people who need a bit of space." She winked.

"Sounds like a kindred spirit, eh, Lucy?" Danny grinned inanely at Elizabeth and rubbed his hands on his jeans. "Er… Would be, erm… Lovely to meet your mum. I mean mums. Ahem. Er… Fancy a drink, Luce?"

"I'll get some Cokes in. I can jump the queue." Danny watched Elizabeth's dark curls bounce off behind the bar.

The 'run away' feeling that had gripped Lucy just a few minutes ago was fading. This was a good place to be. She could see everything happening but wasn't 'in it'. She could hear the conversations, but they weren't next to her, vying for her attention. This was OK. She balled a stray thread from her jumper between her fingers and took some deep breaths. In, out, in, out. This was OK. She watched the new log leak sap onto the flames, bubbling contentedly as the fire curled anew around it.

"Wow." Danny was fidgeting and looking in the direction Elizabeth had gone. "She just knew. Isn't she amazing, Luce?" Lucy could see Danny was besotted already. She smiled.

"Yeah, she's great." The warmth from the fire made her cheeks glow, and she watched as Finn from the Post

Office chatted animatedly to Grandma, making her titter and blush. He saw Lucy looking in their direction and waved from across the room. Her and Danny had helped him clear the shelves earlier, and once he'd found out Lucy's penchant for M&Ms, three huge bags had been thrust into her hands.

A tall lady with a ginger plait caught Lucy's eye from the bar as she wiped a glass with a tea-towel and winked. That must be Elizabeth's mum, Saffy. She recognised the guy from the fair, shirt sleeves shoved to his elbows, sipping a pint and talking animatedly to a guy in a tweed cap. His kids weren't there. They must be at home in bed. This wasn't London. There was no pressure. Everyone talked to everyone else. It didn't matter who you were, what your history was. It felt like this was where she belonged. Lucy wondered if the village had always been this way, or whether it was something to do with the meadow. Whether this pub was called The Hare for a reason, and whether this community knew anything about the meadow. She didn't know. But there was something about this place.

Elizabeth returned, expertly clutching three glasses, ice clinking against the sides. On her back was slung a large guitar case covered in stickers. She placed the glasses carefully on the low table and licked the condensation from her fingers.

"So, your mum just told me you play?"

Danny spluttered his sip of drink. "Er. Erm. Yes, a bit."

"Not just a bit, he's great." Lucy smiled at the drink in her hand. The run away feeling had gone, and she crunched at an ice cube, one of her favourite sensations.

"Well then. You borrow mine." Elizabeth drew a wooden recorder out of her back pocket and waggled it at them. "I'm better with this anyway."

The case was placed on a table, latches clicked open, and a gorgeous-looking steel string was lifted carefully out.

"God, she's perfect," Danny muttered under his breath. Taking the guitar, his fingers automatically started checking the tuning.

"Play an E," he said, and Lucy sat back to let the sounds waft over her.

33

The Sentinels

The following morning was bright, and the water had subsided. Mum was on the phone to the insurance company and Grandma was doing a frantic, if a little pointless, clean and wipe around before her taxi was due. Lucy had already dressed, eaten breakfast and ventured into the garden to place her hands on the mother cherry. She decided then that this was going to be her new routine. To check on the Sentinels, to guard them and care for them, and make sure the fairy circles were intact. There were three that she knew of, the two Cherry trees and the Apple at Ceinwen's cottage, but she just knew there were others. She had passed by a spectacular Oak near the pub last night and had felt sure it was watching her. It was one she would need to visit soon, to introduce herself, and to offer assistance.

"Fancy a wander up to the meadow?" Danny already had his walking boots on, having completely ruined his trainers.

"Definitely!" Lucy needed an excuse to get away from the thrum of the vacuum cleaner, and the possibility that Grandma might hand her a duster.

As they reached the top of the path, the meadow opened up and the scent of cherry blossom floated on the breeze. There in all its splendour was Lucy's new Sentinel tree. She kicked off her wellies and shoved her socks into them. Her toes mingled with the soil, and in her mind she silently greeted the creatures she could sense all around her. She closed her eyes and hummed softly. She located Ceinwen in her invisible cottage kitchen, stirring something potent on the stove. Lucy's blanket was laid carefully over two kitchen chairs, gently washed and drying in the warm room. Ceinwen said she would return it as soon as she could, and that it must be treasured. They would call in later and see how her wounds were healing.

Deeper underground, she sensed Puck, furiously concentrating on a piece of parchment, an ink-tipped feather poised in his fingers. Something political with the Council, she was sure of it, and she smiled to herself.

"So what'ya gonna do later?" Danny's long legs loped up the incline with ease, while Lucy cantered beside him. She thought briefly, and then replied,

"I think I might unpack those boxes in my room."

Danny threw his head back and laughed loud into the sky.

"You've decided you're staying, then?" His chuckle continued as he winked at her.

Lucy giggled and spun around, her arms out wide slicing through the cold air and she pranced on her toes.

Danny watched her spinning, relishing the easy smile on her face after all this time. "Saffy and Jo offered me a job, you know, Luce."

Lucy stopped spinning. "Really? That's great!"

"Yeah. It's just a couple of shifts behind the bar, but they do a music night every Saturday and they want me to help plan them out."

"Isn't that sort of what Mum does?"

Danny chuckled. "Never thought of that. Maybe I'm more like her than I thought! Although I was hoping to do more making music than planning events for other people to play at."

Lucy looked at his chin. Her eyes sparkled and her hair was loose, cast away from her face in the spring breeze. "But it's music, at least."

"Yes. It's music. It's a start." She was right, of course. All this time he had been trying to get to the top of the ladder without stepping on the first rung.

"Come with me, Danny, I want to show you something." He followed her up the slope as she ran across the waving grass to place both hands on the bark of the Cherry. His hands were in his pockets and his hair played around his forehead.

Puck had talked about the Balance. The equalness of the world. Nature's ebb and flow, birth and death. Lucy had only half understood it at the time, but now, in this small unassuming meadow, she felt it. The calm. The symmetry. And she breathed it in. Took it into her lungs and let the feeling spread through her veins. The earth below her, the sky above her, the chill of the breeze and the warmth of the sun. The boughs of the Cherry reached protectively out over their heads, and she felt the roots buried deep beneath her. Everything was righted.

"I still can't believe you grew this." Danny gazed up unto the boughs and closed his eyes as a couple of petals dislodged and brushed his cheek on their descent, as if to acknowledge him.

"That's not all I can do." Danny's eyes widened as Lucy grinned, shut her eyes tight, stuck her fingers in her ears, and thought, 'mole'.

Lightning Source UK Ltd.
Milton Keynes UK
UKHW012320071020
371175UK00003B/104